BIG BROTHER,

Little Sister

To Charli

Enjoy!

Elena S♥

by
Elena Southworth

Elena Southworth
www.prodigykidspress.com

Publisher's Note: This is a work of fiction. Names, characters, places, and incidents are a product of the author's imagination. Locales and public names are sometimes used for atmospheric purposes. Any resemblance to actual people, living or dead, or to businesses, companies, events, institutions, or locales is completely coincidental.

Book design: TheBookMakers.com

Big Brother, Little Sister / Elena Southworth — First Edition
Print ISBN: 978-1-7357829-0-4
eBook ISBN: 978-1-7357829-1-1

For Mason, my LB

Look out world!

The Harpers are ready to tell their story!

contents

1

Big Brother, Little Sister

MATTHeW

"Please, Mom! Just take Aaliyah to a friend's house or something! It's the only day I have to go and get a suit for the dance—" But I don't get to finish my sentence. I never do.

"It's only for an hour, Matthew. She won't bother you."

Of course. Aaliyah is now my priority. Again.

Oops! Sorry! I got so distracted with trying to convince Mom not to leave me with the worst sister in space and time that I forgot to introduce myself. My name is Matthew Harper. I guess I consider myself an ordinary high school kid. I mean, I get my homework done and then go play video games for as long as possible. I would love a spicy tuna roll during math class, and I spent a good amount of time looking for the perfect girl to ask out to the end-of-the-year school dance, which is happening in three weeks. The same girl I went to prom with. *Delaney.* I go to football practice after school and basketball practice on Saturdays. I like to watch baseball games on the TV and eat potato chips.

I live in Downtown Las Vegas. The big city in the middle of a flaming-hot desert. My house is two stories, and there are only three bedrooms and two and a half bathrooms. It is not big or fancy, but the fact that I call it "home" is all I need.

I have two sisters. One of them is older than me, and the other is younger. Camille is in college at Wagon Wheel University. She was three or four when I was born. I never minded her. Cami definitely wasn't your typical big sister. I could never remember her picking on me, and we rarely got into fights. Every time we did, it was my fault. I have to admit that.

I don't see Cami much anymore, and we aren't very close like we used to be. Cami isn't my only sister. I have a younger one as well. Aaliyah. She is only eight.

You wouldn't think we are related. I am awesome and cool and smart, and superior to her. She is annoying and dumb and rude. We don't even look anything like siblings! I have blonde hair. Surprisingly, I don't have any freckles, even though everyone else in my family does. Aaliyah, on the other hand, has shiny auburn hair that is stick straight and down her back. She has bangs and glacier blue eyes.

She is nothing like Cami. She's crazy, bossy, mean, and she blames everything she does on someone else. Whether it's me, Cami, or a kid at school. She gets away with everything by bending the truth.

Aaliyah has never changed. From the day she was born, she's always been the mean girl. Unless it's someone she actually likes, she's a total brat.

To make matters worse, Aaliyah has more friends than *anyone* I know or have ever met. She puts on a nice face. She's good at it, too. Aaliyah acts like a very friendly and outgoing person. She has so many friends I've lost count of them. From normal kids at school to adults to animals to even the little critters that creep around inside the bottom slit of our tire swing, you name it! Aaliyah is friends with them all. Little two-face.

Aaliyah has this thing where every time somebody says, "Aaliyah," she needs to say, "That's my name!" It drives me crazy. Crazy!

I was about nine when mom brought Aaliyah into the world. She has been the absolute golden child from day one and even before that! I remember being at Mom's dumb and boring baby shower. So fancy. Mom sat in a basket of flower petals, a gigantic ribbon tied around her belly. There were cupcakes and chocolate fountains with strawberries and dozens of guests. About a week after Aaliyah was born, something was done for her called a celebration of life, which I thought was done when someone died! Guess not.

All that happened at that dumb party was a bunch of chanting while Aaliyah laid in a fancy crib with a canopy, totally asleep. All of us kids were bored and watching the clock, waiting for it to be over. *I kinda wish it was for death,* I remember thinking after the first hour of the "celebration" of life.

Mom and Dad did not do things like that for Cami and I. Aaliyah's first birthday was held in a castle in Rome. For crying out loud! 15 guests were invited, and almost everybody (13 of them) came! I was appalled. I mean, come on! That may not sound like a lot of people, but who is going to fly to Rome to watch a filthy baby eat cake? That is still vivid in my mind, even if it was over seven years ago when I was ten and scrawny. The PTSD of that unbearably boring party still haunts me to this day.

According to Mom, Dad, Cami, and a few photos, *my* first birthday was in the backyard. Only family and a few friends had been invited. Nobody even showed up. I just sat there in my applesauce-stained highchair and poked at a small vanilla mush cake. Sigh. *That's probably why Mom chose a Roman castle for the next one,* I like to believe.

Cami's first birthday was at a park. And I think hers was worse than mine. The only guests were Mom, Dad, and my old grandmas... Grandma Pearl and Grandma Agnes. One with a walker and the other with a cane. My grandpas didn't even go. The playground was not even available because there was construction going on to put in a new big toy, since the current one was so bad! There is an old picture on the mantle of it. In that picture, Cami is crying in the grass, a tractor in the background. It was a joke. Our mantle is covered in a trillion pictures, by the way. It's really cluttered, but other than that, we are pretty organized people. Only three of those pictures are of me, and two are Cami's. I bet you can guess who the rest are pictures of? Mom even hangs up *drawings* Aaliyah makes! All over the fresh white paint on our walls! A big TAPESTRY of Aaliyah's FACE hangs over the couch. I know! One time, Aaliyah wrote her name in cursive on an old sheet of math homework. Mom framed it! The "photo" still hangs in the same spot.

My life hasn't been the same ever since the birth of my little sister. Aaliyah is a pretty happy kid in general, other than when something bad is going on. Sometimes she can be a little bit too positive and adventurous, though. It usually leads to a crazy adventure. We like to call all of our unbelievable adventures *BBLS*, which stands for: Big Brother, Little Sister. It's a thing we've had for a while. With us, *every day* is an adventure. Here's our story from different views.

Aaliyah

Matthew says I'm annoying. I don't think I am, and I definitely don't try to be, unless he's mad. I love to make people feel even worse. It's just so funny. I'm good at it, too. With years of experience under my belt, I know all the little tricks. I know what people can't stand.

We have this thing called BBLS: Big Brother, Little Sister. He says big brothers are great and little sisters are just annoying, gross, rude, a waste of time, and completely in the way of everything. But in his eyes, I'll always be unable to do anything right. Always be a chatterbox of useless ideas. Always be younger. That younger part is true, I guess, but I think he's just angry that Mom makes him watch me like a hawk twenty-four seven. Dad doesn't care. He always lets Mom win. He's probably the laziest person ever. He's as lazy as Mom is hyper. That's just my parents Mike and Tammy Harper for you. Sigh.

Matthew may not realize this now, but he annoys me, too. I'm eight years old and mature for my age, or so Mom says. Oh, and by the way, Mom is infuriating when it comes to me. She thinks I am so innocent. I never get in trouble. Not that I like getting in trouble or anything. It's just embarrassing how she has to call me an innocent little angel everywhere we go and something happens. People stare, laugh, and point.

If what Mom says about me being mature or whatever is true, then I don't think I need my bully-of-a-brother to be a babysitter for me so much. Once a week would be fine with me.

It's not like I get into much trouble, right? Right????

Camille

From the time I was a kid, my goal in life has been to become a teacher. Fourth grade, preferably. I would love teaching young minds about the gold rush and long division. That goal will be accomplished soon, as this is my last year of college until I move on to get my teaching credential.

I have always loved kids. They can definitely be troublesome, though. I have a little brother. He isn't so little anymore, though! Seventeen. I also have a little sister. She actually is little...

My graduation from college happened a few days ago. Get this: Only Dad and Matthew came. My little sister, Aaliyah, didn't come for whatever reason. I don't know why. Mom had to stay back with "The Baby." This annoys me so much.

I've really been hoping that my family has outgrown this phase. I will be coming home from college in a few weeks and will be staying with all of them. I won't get my hopes up too high, though, because that's what I've been wishing for for years, and I get disappointed every time.

2

Shaka Shaka

MATTHEW

A few weeks before the last day of school, Aaliyah and I were getting ready for school when we heard the news.

"Kids," Mom shrieked in her annoying, squeaky voice. "With summer break starting in just less than a month, we have made plans." Aaliyah and I looked at each other. What was going on?

"To prevent lazy days and to celebrate Matthew's high school graduation and eighteenth birthday, we are going on a tropical vacation to Hawaii for three weeks in August! We will snorkel, swim with dolphins, go diving, climb some very high rock walls, eat seafood dinners at a five-star restaurant, and stay in a luxury hotel! And get this: Camille will be coming with us, as she is returning from college for the summer!"

I couldn't believe my ears! I'm not sure how much of that is true (I mean, this was coming from Mom,) but I was so excited that I could barely concentrate at school. I even started practicing my Shaka wave!

Aaliyah

I've only got to live with Camille for four years. Not very long, for siblings. Even before she left for college, we still weren't super close because she was a teenager, and I was just a very little kid. She was always busy with something, and I didn't care. I don't think she loved me very much. It sure never seemed like it.

I wasn't sure what to say when I found out we would be traveling together for more than a couple days. Every time we would go on those family vacations, they would only last a few days. I was about four when she left for college. Before that, I was too little to stay in places away from home for a long amount of time. Big bummer. I just hope she's not like Matthew.

MATTHEW

Whew! What a great way to celebrate my graduation! When Aaliyah was born, we stopped going on vacation, and we didn't start back up again until she was six or seven. But by then, Cami was in college and things weren't the same. It's never the same without Cami.

I was so excited for this trip that, I had trouble sleeping, but for no reason I could figure, Aaliyah didn't seem thrilled.

At school, I told Delaney, my girlfriend and dance date, about our trip to Maui.

"Wow," Delaney says. "Matthew, that's so cool!" We talked for a little longer, and then the bell rang and we went to our classes. I've known Delaney since first grade. We grew up together. We didn't become a "thing" (or even talk to each other) until December this year. About halfway through my first period class, an announcement is said over the loudspeaker.

"*Matthew Harper,*" Principal Reedy's voice blares over right into our ears. "*Please come to my office as soon as possible. We need to talk to you and then bring you down to the elementary playground.*"

I began to worry. Had I done something wrong? Or was it another Aaliyah problem? Hmmm . . .

Aaliyah

Matthew and I go to the same school called Cactus City School. Our mascot, as strange as it may sound, is a...cactus. Yep. It starts with Kindergarten through 5th grade in one building then middle school and high school in a separate building on another campus. They are all within walking distance. We never see each other there, except when Matthew drives us to and from school in his car. Before Matthew learned to drive, we used to ride the bus, which I absolutely despised. It smelled like feet, and the driver was as grumpy as Dad.

Me, Kate, Bria, and Lizzy were playing on the monkey bars. We were doing a competition on who could go across the fastest. I was winning up until Kate jumped to the other side and was ahead of me.

"Haha, Aaliyah!" Kate zoomed up, getting closer and closer to the end. So I decided to do the same thing she did, and jump to the other side.

Bad idea. My hands slipped and I started to fall. I tried grasping another bar below me with my feet. It worked, but just for a second. I fell, landing directly on my ankle. I could hear it as it snapped. Supervisors came running over, and one of them even called an ambulance! It was the worst pain I had ever felt. I saw Matthew walk out of the office, holding his phone that he isn't supposed to have during school hours.

The sound of sirens and my own screaming filled my ears. Paramedics picked me up, put me on a stretcher, and spoke to Matthew. They hauled the stretcher into the ambulance, shut the doors, and started driving away to the emergency room. It was so entertaining! I always wanted to ride in an ambulance, but I couldn't enjoy it much because my foot hurt. What I did see was cool, though. As we drove out of the school parking lot, I looked back at Cactus City School and saw the pinched faces of my friends.

MATTHEW

Aaliyah fell off the monkey bars, which is what I found out when I got down to the playground. A supervisor called 911. They asked me to call Mom on my personal phone. The ambulance arrived as I was telling her about what I knew.

"Actually, just go to the hospital now. Don't worry about getting me. School will be over in a few hours. I'll drive myself there after. Delaney and I are supposed to hang out today, but I'll just reschedule." Mom told me I could bring Delaney. I hung up and got back to class.

3

Scaredy Dog

Delaney

Matthew told me about his sister. Poor thing. I've ridden in an ambulance before. It smells awful. I have a little sister, too. Her name is Mindy. She's nine and very annoying. Matthew and I both think they should meet each other so that, instead of bothering us constantly, they could play together. When school was over, I rode with Matthew on the bus back to his house, where we jumped on Aaliyah's bed like little kids for ten minutes, and then drove the car to the hospital. Matthew told me that jumping on Aaliyah's bed was better than jumping on his because Aaliyah would have to clean it up, not us.

When we arrived at the hospital and parked the car, Matthew totally humiliated me. So, some old man was walking out of the hospital, his dog on a leash walking next to him. When we walked by, the dog started barking. Matthew totally freaked out. How embarrassing! But it gets worse. He jumped up onto my back, the entire parking lot staring at us. I hid my face in my jacket, trying not to draw attention. A few people from the waiting room and entrance of the hospital poked their heads out to see what all the commotion was about. Still screaming, Matthew jumped off of my back and started running for dear life. I tried everything I could to not look like I knew him. The dog was still barking, too. I guess he wasn't looking where he was going because he tripped over a bench and fell right into the trash can. The trash can was discombobulated. By then, everybody was looking. The dog started barking again. And Matthew started up his entire acting-like-a-chicken-having-a-seizure Broadway show again.

"Delaney, it's looking me straight in the eye!" I buried my face in my jacket once more.

"Let's just go inside and check in." And that's how I ended up giving my boyfriend a piggyback ride into the hospital to visit his eight-year-old sister who had suffered a terrible accident, all because he was scared of a dog.

MATTHEW

"*What* is wrong with you?!" Delaney harshly whispered to me as we walked in. I've been terrified of dogs ever since I was a little kid walking to school and got attacked by a stray one. I was seven years old and had to go to the hospital. I bled quite a lot for three days straight.

"We are here to visit Aaliyah Harper," I told the secretary at the front desk when we were checking in.

"And what relationships do you two have with her?" she asked.

"I'm her brother, Matthew, and this is my girlfriend Delaney Emerson." The secretary nods.

"Ah, yes. Your mom put your names at the desk. She is in room #419. Thank you." She handed us both a sticker to wear on our shirts that had some boring hospital information on it. We got in the elevator and made our way up to Aaliyah's room. Before entering, Delaney walked down the hall to the gift shop and bought flowers and a balloon for Aaliyah.

Aaliyah

I think I might have fallen asleep in the ambulance before arriving at the hospital. When I did wake up, I saw Matthew, Mom, and Matthew's girlfriend, Delaney, sitting in metal chairs on the other side of the room. Matthew was reading comics, Mom was on her phone, and Delaney was eating a protein bar and watching TV. I was lying on a mattress that was highly elevated from the floor. A red balloon was tied to the edge of the bed. My eyes were barely open when I noticed that my leg was tied up high to some sort of wrap thing that connected to the ceiling. As I opened my eyes a little more, I realized something strange. My foot was very thick, and almost . . . blue?

"Mom," I say a little louder than I intended to. She looked up. "What is going on with my foot? Where am I? How long have I been asleep?" But Mom doesn't need to answer my question because, just then, the doctor walked in. He was carrying a huge stack of paperwork that was attached to a clipboard. I saw the top paper. It looked like an X-ray, but very busted up. Oh boy. That was my foot, misplaced and broken. And I could tell by the look on his face, there wasn't great news.

"So, in the X-ray, it showed how her foot was clearly broken. She has a blood clot and will need surgery to drain it out. She'll be out of action for weeks. We will have to put her in a cast and give her a wheelchair. Don't let her go anywhere without the wheelchair. Doing so can re-injure her. Eventually, she could start using crutches. Oh, and I see she's awake." Still drowsy, I asked what was going on.

"Aaliyah,"

"That's my name," I said. I braced myself for what was coming next.

"You have a bad break," he explained to me. *Well duh, -* I thought to myself. My foot hurt so bad. There was numbness throughout my leg. Nobody spoke. I finally broke the silence by asking Mom a question that I was suspenseful to find out the answer to.

"Mom, can we still go to Hawaii?" Her and the doctor exchanged looks.

"Well," she started. "It depends. We will probably go a lot later in the summer, depending on how you are doing and how long it takes your foot to heal. You have been asleep for about three or four hours. While you slept, the doctors did some scans on you to see what the diagnosis is. Keep it elevated. You will have to stay here for a day or two to have surgery."

Ughhhhhhh! This is *so* unsatisfying! My entire summer is now down the drain!

Delaney

Matthew and I were sent home. The next day, first thing in the morning, Aaliyah would undergo foot surgery. We decided to make her bed for her. She's had enough issues. After hanging out for a little while at his house, he drove me back to mine.

During the car ride, Matthew told me about why he was so paranoid about dogs. He said it was a phobia called Cynophobia, or fear of dogs. These problems sounded a lot like it.

I got out of the car and started walking towards my house, but then something terrible happened. A dog started running down the street. I was on my porch, and Matthew was in the car. The car... was still on. Then of course - of *course* the dog had to start jumping on the doors of the car. And of course, Matthew had to leave the window open. The dog jumped inside the car and I ran over to take it out, but I was too late. Matthew screamed. He hit the gas pedal and took off. Neighbors started running out of their houses.

The car went zooming down the busy city road as I was telling each neighbor to just go about their business. Someone even asked me if I wanted them to call the police. They pulled out their phone.

"No, it's just a little incident. Some dog just jumped into the car," I tell him.

"Was it a stray?" he asks.

"I have no idea. But everything is okay." Matthew skids across the cul-de-sac, and the dog finally jumped out of the window. Jeez. I picked it up and put it on the sidewalk. Matthew stops the car, and I say good-bye.

I don't want to tell him about the massive dent on the side door. He'll figure it out on his own soon enough.

4

Madness in the Mall

Aaliyah

Today was the day I had surgery. The doctors put
medicine in me to make me fall asleep. I kept thinking to
myself that it'll be over soon, but the fact that they were
basically going to twist my foot back into place kinda scared
me.

"Okay, Aaliyah, just close your eyes. It will be over before
you know it. You are sick and we are going to make you
better." One of the doctors told me that. So I did what he
told me. I closed my eyes, and I was asleep into thin air.

MATTHEW

Aaliyah came home from the hospital yesterday. She had a cast on and was in a wheelchair. Her leg was elevated, with an icepack covering her toes. She was in a very sour mood. Aaliyah is usually a pretty happy kid, like I said, but definitely not now! Mom, Dad, and just about everyone who we know is spoiling her rotten. I feel a little sorry for her, but, since she will be out of action, at least nothing bad could happen now!

That was true up until she had been home for about three hours, and Mom and Dad told us to get in the car. We were going to the mall for dinner and to buy Aaliyah another new toy.

"You can get something too, bud." Dad said, briefly opening his eyes and nudging me. *Great.* Wait . . . hold on. No way! Dad actually spoke, let alone, opened his eyes?! I'm shocked.

I was glad that she didn't have her legs to do anything.

But no matter what happens, *BBLS* stuff is always going to follow us.

Aaliyah

I woke up. I didn't remember having any of the surgery, but my leg felt terrible, and I had a bad headache. After sleeping for a little while longer in my hospital bed, Mom went downstairs and got me a wheelchair. It was tiny, yellow, and said *kidz wheelz* on the side. Everywhere you looked on it, there was some sort of rainbow or smiley face. I guess it was supposed to cheer me up. It didn't.

A few days later, the doctors cleared me to go home. We thanked the doctor, grabbed all of my personal belongings, and left the hospital. When we got home, there was a pile of toys and gifts sitting in my room.

"These are from friends and some neighbors, but we'll open them when we get back. Get in the car! We're going out to dinner at the mall!" Dad then got mad and had a fight with Mom.

"Dinner? Tammy, she just got out of the hospital! Don't you think she should be resting?" I do have to say, Dad did make a point, but I'm not really the stay at home type. I like eating out. It's fun! So we just went anyway. After all, Dad really couldn't care less.

We were getting into Mom's car, but then decided to use Matthew's car instead because it was higher on gas. We noticed a humongous dent on the door. Mom and Dad totally freaked out. Matthew swore to all of us that he had no clue where it came from.

"I don't know where it's from! Really! I'm a good driver! I didn't do it!" But he still got in huge trouble.

"We expect more from you, Matthew James," Mom started.

"That car was a lot of money! Now we either spend a lot more money on getting it fixed, or we leave it there forever!" Dad screamed. Then it went back to mom.

"Make a choice. But, either way, you are in big trouble!"
Matthew just looked down. It was great! I tried so hard not
to laugh!

"I can't pay to get it fixed. All that money I saved up is to
buy myself a suit for the dance. We could wait until I save
up again." Mom and Dad nodded. We got into the car and
drove over to the mall.

MATTHEW

I feel like I do know a little bit about the dent. When the
dog jumped into my car back at Delaney's house, I sped
around the street and the side of the car hit a gate door. I'm
guilty . . .

We took the big glass elevator up to the restaurant,
which was on the third floor! It cheered me up from the car
dent incident.

We stood in line, waiting to check in. It was so long that
it almost went toward the escalator. We were the very last
ones, right at the back. None of us knew that Aaliyah's
wheelchair didn't have the breaks on. It started rolling
backwards, and the next thing we knew, Aaliyah and her
wheelchair were rolling down the escalator. Mom, who was
having a heart attack, pressed the emergency stop button,
and I slid down the railing trying to grab her. Some of the
other people who were on there grabbed her arms and legs,
trying furiously to stop her from falling all the way down.
One man undid the seat belt and was able to take her out.
Whew. Disaster avoided. I let out a huge sigh of relief.

Aaliyah was okay! The wheelchair, on the other hand, was not. It kept on rolling. It was thrown from the escalator with great force. It hit a table where some woman was selling phone cases and continued to skid across the white tile floor. The wheelchair went tumbling out the door. People ran after it to try and stop it.

That's not the end of it! Still on the rail to the escalator, my hand slipped. I started it back up again. Aaliyah, who was sitting on the step and hadn't said a word all night, couldn't get up because of her leg. Her dress got stuck.

"Aaaahhh! Help me!" Aaliyah screamed and kicked and hit things. People grabbed her waist. I raced to the top and pushed the emergency stop button again. It was madness!

Aaliyah

It's not my fault I almost died! However, I still got in a tremendous amount of trouble. When will I catch a break?

MATTHEW

Aaliyah could not get unstuck. Someone who worked there had to come and cut her dress. Aaliyah's brand-new purple dress . . . was now a rag. We put Aaliyah back in her wheelchair, cleaned up the mess, and left without dinner or toys.

Mom and Dad did not have good things to say to us.

"First the dent in the car, and now this? Aaliyah, how did you not know that your brakes weren't on? It's your job to take care of that. All you have to do is reach down and press it. And Matthew, we know that your intentions were good, but you could've been a lot less obnoxious! Two bad things in just a night. The time for adventures that cause inconveniences is now over." Mom said. Dad wasn't as nice about it. He never is.

"You are both going to suffer consequences! Aaliyah, you don't get to open any of those presents until you can prove to us that you are responsible enough to put the brake on your wheelchair and also responsible enough not to be doing foolish things like messing around on monkey bars without caution and having accidents! And Matthew, it is time that you have learned how to act like a 17-year-old and not be obnoxious and rude. No more crazy driving so that you won't put another dent in the car that we bought for you! If one more thing that your Mom and I or anyone else isn't happy about happens, then we are going to take away your tickets to Hawaii and just go by ourselves with Camille. Understood?"

We nod our heads. We've just gotta make sure that Aaliyah won't do anything stupid until our trip is over. But the trip is still a while away, and that may not be humanly possible.

Aaliyah

"Great job, genius," Matthew tells me as we are brushing our teeth that night.

"I don't know what everyone is so annoyed about! I almost died because of you! Everything would have been fine if you hadn't totally started up the escalator again!"

"I started it up by accident!" Matthew grunts and walks to his room. I wheel myself back to mine. My room is right next to his.

I yell through the wall, "And I fell down by accident." He doesn't respond, but he definitely heard it. I park my wheelchair in the spot next to my nightstand, right where I keep it. I stack some pillows and then elevate my foot onto them. I turn out my light and close my eyes. I think about everything that has happened to me in the past two weeks. I killed my foot, had surgery, fell down an escalator in my wheelchair, got stuck, and I am still dealing with my mean, worthless big brother. Thank goodness I don't have anything going on tomorrow. I fell asleep.

5

Makeup Mischief

MATTHEW

Today was the day to get my dance suit! I started to feel better about the dent. My phone dinged. It was Delaney. She said she got her dress the other night. I quickly ate breakfast and then hurried out to the car. The day was going to be perfect! Only then, Mom stopped me.

"Wait! Matthew!" She walked up to the front of the window and explained the horrific news.

"Look, bud. I need to go to work. You know what that means," she giggled nervously.

"No, Mom! Please don't make me bring Aaliyah! Her wheelchair is impossible to bring anywhere, and she would just do nothing but annoy me and get in my way! You could easily just hire a babysitter," I replied.

Mom says nothing. I knew that she didn't want to pay for one. She goes back inside. I continued back to my phone and talked to Delaney a little bit. Then I hear a sassy, sharp voice.

"Hiiiiii, Matthew!" Aaliyah sits in her wheelchair, Mom standing beside. They both have these huge smiles on their faces. It's like they're on a team, both ganging up to annoy me. Aaliyah crosses her legs, then bats her eyelashes like some sort of domesticated skunk! Her hair is tied up in a bun that has an enormous silver bow latched onto it, and she wears a checkered blue T-shirt with pink biker shorts. Her bangs have even been freshly combed and trimmed. What a show-off! Aaliyah hums some hideous tune as Mom lifts her from her bright yellow wheelchair and puts her on top of her dirty purple booster seat. What an annoyance! Then Mom opens the trunk and THROWS the wheelchair in! *She's worried about the dent?! That thing could do more damage than I ever could.*

"Bye-bye, Mommy!!!" Aaliyah rolls down the window and screams loud enough for the whole continent to hear. Then she giggles. What a weirdo! She's definitely doing all this just to annoy me. I look behind and give her a death stare. She looks back at me, confidently. Then raises an eyebrow.

Aaliyah

It feels *so* good to annoy Matthew! I never actually try to be annoying in general, but when someone is angry, I never miss a chance. When we finally pull up to the mall, something incredible happens! Matthew tries to take out my wheelchair from the trunk, but then falls! He grunts the way that every annoying teenager does when they are being lazy. Teenagers are always lazy, by the way. That was when Matthew literally topples over! His butt sticks up in the air, and I could actually see a little bit of his smelly white underwear! Yes! I love it! It was so great! I could not stop laughing. I felt proud, as well. Matthew grabs me by the arms and straps me into the *Kidz Wheelz*. None of it would have happened if it weren't for *my* wheelchair. BBLS, to be honest with you, would be absolutely nothing if there wasn't a little sister involved.

MATTHEW

It has not been a good day to start with and then something unbelievably horrific happens when we get in the shop.

"Hello," I say to the salesperson. She looks up and smiles. "I am here to get a suit to wear to a school dance. I want something that's classy and sharp, but not too 'Heyyy, look and me,' all packed into one." The salesperson leads me over to an aisle containing some affordable clothes that might be possibilities.

"Aaliyah," I yell at her. "You may go wheel yourself over to the makeup area. You may try on some testers but on one condition. Don't come out looking like a clown." Aaliyah is beaming. She likes makeup.

"Okay! Thank you so much, Matthew!" I watch Aaliyah, who is smiling from ear to ear, wheel herself over to the makeup section.

Aaliyah

This is the coolest day of my life! I get to put on as much makeup as I want! As I sit in my wheelchair in front of makeup, I just get fascinated by the dozens of different brands for dozens of different types of makeup. It's all on a four story shelf. A sign with circle lights that said *Samples* was on the top shelf. Too bad I can only reach the bottom shelf in my wheelchair. I grab a brush and a palette of eyeshadow. I gently dab some on. *Strange, there's a seal.* Then I squirt foundation onto my face and rub it in with a shiny pink sponge. Now onto lipstick! I take it out of its container. Fresh and pointy with a little red tint. Lovely! I continue breaking the seals of gloss, mascara, eye liner, and even glittery stuff that I sprinkle onto my arms. Cool! I even spray on some perfume. Through the corner of my eye, I can see salespeople watching me.

"Kid," said one of the men who was working as a salesperson. Another lady asked me to point to my mommy or daddy. Then the salesperson continued:

"Now what is it you're doing?"

MATTHEW

Oh. My. Oh no . . . Aaliyah Jasmine Harper, you are going to meet your grave today. Aaliyah was being spoken to by some salespeople. She tried on makeup and surprisingly looked okay. But there was still another problem that was so big and would cost a really, *really* big amount of money.

"Aaliyah . . ." I say, trying everything possible to start breathing again. I was going into septic shock.

"That's my name . . ." she chuckled nervously.

"Aaliyah. Those. Aren't. Samples!!!!!"

Aaliyah replied, "They are samples! See, there is a sign right above this shelf that says 'samples.' They must be." She is so dumb.

"The testers are on the top of the shelf! Those were the actual products!" I explained that to Aaliyah.

"Ohhh. Yeah. I did think it was a little weird that they were all sealed." I talked to the salespeople, and Aaliyah just sat in her wheelchair toying with the colored leather on it.

"I'm so sorry," said the salesperson. "But the total cost for this is going to be $106.46. You could pay with cash or debit." I tried not to scream. My suit was $75. And I only had $118. Aaliyah is as poor as a hobo (she has 45 cents in her allowance), so that wouldn't make a dent. I couldn't make her pay. So I cashed in the hard-earned money. What am I supposed to wear to the dance now? My prom suit, maybe, but it just seemed better to get something clean and new. I know I still have that, and that I should just wear it, but that's not the point. That was my money that I worked hard for, it shouldn't be wasted by Aaliyah. It was all her fault! We went home without saying a word.

Aaliyah

When Mom and Dad found out about this one, it was just game over for Matthew and I. Especially me.

There was a whole ton of screaming going on when we got home. Mom actually wasn't too mad at me but Dad was. Mom never gets mad at me. It's always Matthew getting in trouble with her. However, Mom did offer to buy Matthew a suit. After all, it was his money, and he didn't have very much to do with the problem other than letting me put makeup on without Mom's permission. I don't like being in trouble, but I still do have something to look forward to. Two days from now, I get rid of my wheelchair and start using crutches instead!

MATTHEW

Mom and I pull up in the parking lot to the mall the next afternoon. She is going to give me back the money that I lost all because of Aaliyah! We walk over to the same suit that I have been eyeing. Mom buys it for me.

"I'm sorry, bud," Mom starts saying as we check out. "It really isn't your fault. I've just been so annoyed lately. You and your sister, I just have no idea what has gotten into you guys." Honestly, I don't either. Then I explained to her the meaning of BBLS.

"It's something that Aaliyah and I made up a few years ago. It stands for: Big Brother Little Sister. A little cheesy, but it makes sense I guess."

We drove back to the house. On the way, I felt great to have something to wear.

Aaliyah

The sound of morning filled my ears. Birds chirped at my window and bacon sizzled in a frying pan. I felt nothing but relaxed. Up until I realized what day it was. Forget about being relaxed—today I'm getting out of my wheelchair! I mean, I still have to wear a cast, and I need crutches, but at least I could get around without being completely helpless! As a bonus to that, school gets out in three days! But I get to skip today because I'm seeing the doctor again. Matthew is going to the dance tomorrow. So, I get an entire day without him! Hallelujah! Things are finally looking up!

MATTHEW

Delaney comes up to me today when I am at my locker. She has a happy face.

"Matthew," she said. "I am so excited for the dance tomorrow. How's Aaliyah doing? Maybe I could come by after school today?" I opened my mouth to say something, but Principal Reedy ran into us and spoke first.

"Matthew Harper and Delaney Emerson," he says. He seemed happy, though. "Just who I'm looking for. Follow me into my office. I need to ask you both something."

6

Airport Awfulness

Camille

I said good-bye to Lisa, my roommate, and left for the airport. Today, college ended, and I would be going back home for the summer. I got onto my plane, and about twenty minutes later, it started. But then, before even being lifted from the ground, it stopped. Huh? People were going a little crazy. Then, an announcement came over the loudspeaker.

"Those of you on this plane, Galaxy Carriers, flight seventeen to Downtown Las Vegas, must unboard. There has been a delay due to some extremely high turbulence

levels detected on the way. We are sorry about the inconvenience."

Boarding off the plane was just mayhem. There were so many angry passengers. It was total chaos in the airport, and nobody was listening to directions. To make things worse, the pilot then got sick. He was vomiting and had a high fever all of a sudden. The flight was delayed *again*! An emergency pilot from another carrier had to come and take his place, but it took him nearly an hour to actually get here.

Then, things got even worse. Right as I was giving the attendant my suitcase, I realized that it was the wrong one. *Michael Nassar* was on the name tag. It wasn't Camille Harper at all. This Michael dude must have had the same one and taken it instead of taking his! I had to find it. It contained my MacBook, some study textbooks and work, and clothing. Too valuable to give up. I'm sure he felt the same way. I explained my dilemma to the attendee and said I needed to go, then went to the front desk to see if somehow we could find it. Takeoff was in three minutes! I needed to do this quickly! And then, to my surprise, a man holding a little boy walked up, wheeling the same baby blue suitcase that was mixed up with one just like it.

"Hello, I think my suitcase got mixed up with yours since you are carrying the exact same one. Are you Camille?" I let out a sigh of relief so big I thought I would faint.

"That's me! Here you go," I say to him. We switch back to our own suitcases. Right when I think that everything's finally okay, the worst thing of all happens. My flight . . . has already left. Without me.

Aaliyah

Mom pushes me into the doctor's office. I'm so excited! The doctor does a few X-rays and then tells us the results.

"Wow, Aaliyah. Your foot is healing very well; you're very resilient. You may start using crutches now! But you must take it easy and keep your foot off the ground. Keep ice packs on it as much as possible, and it should heal soon." We leave and go down to the pharmacy where I get my crutches. They are small, pink, and specially designed for kids.

"Aaliyah, these could not be more perfect for you!" Mom says. I myself am amused. After practicing on them for a while, we go home and ice it.

A few hours later, Matthew gets back from school. Next to him is Delaney, and next to her is a girl about my age. She looks similar to Delaney.

"Aaliyah," Delaney says to me. "I want you to meet my sister, Mindy. She is nine and in third grade, a year older than you." Mindy waves at me. I smile and wave back.

"But Delaney says that she is just as annoying as you are, Aaliyah!" Matthew shouts loud enough for the entire city to hear. Delaney gives him a playful punch. Then, Mom leaves to go and run her errands.

"I will be in third grade next year," I say. Me and Mindy go outside to the playhouse that I've gotten too big for.

"I have a good idea," Mindy tells me. "We play a prank on Matthew and Delaney!"

"Yes! I totally agree! But what would we do?" Then Mindy explains it to me. We laugh so hard we almost die.

MATTHEW

Principal Reedy brings us into his office. Delaney asks him what is going on and why we were there.

"Aaliyah's second grade teacher, Mrs. Greyson, told me that the class is having a surprise party for her on the last day of school. You two have been invited to help out," he says.

"Okay," I say. "That is cool of them."

Mr. Reedy dismissed us back to class. Though it was a nice idea, I knew that something BBLS-oriented was going to happen.

Camille

"Are you sure there is nothing before then?" I ask the lady. She starts typing furiously at the computer once more. I listened to the click of her horrific, pointy fake nails. *How does she wipe her butt with those things?*

"Sorry ma'am, but the soonest flight we've got to Las Vegas is tomorrow evening. Everything else is booked. There may be one by another carrier, but the nearest carrier is two hours away at least. And according to my computer, they don't have anything for a while, either. To fly with us, you would have to find a hotel to stay in."

"Well, do you know how long it'd take to maybe drive there, to Vegas?" I asked her, even though I already knew the answer.

"Fourteen hours," she frowns. So do I. As miserable as that sounded, I decided just to do it. I didn't want to spend money on a hotel, or drive to a different carrier just to find out that they have no flights available. I packed up my car and started driving. Only fourteen hours of hot and rural desert to go before reaching the city, all the way in Downtown Las Vegas, Nevada. Vegas itself was a desert, too.

Just what was I thinking?

Delaney

I heard the little girls' voices outside Matthew's door. We listened carefully.

"Delaney! Matthew! A dog ran into the house! Come quick! It's about to break into your room!"

"No, there is not! Leave us alone!" I scream. But Matthew totally believes them. He runs out of the room but trips on something. Oh for goodness' sake. He falls right on his belly and then slides all the way across the hallway.

I take a look at the thing on the doorway. It's a string. Then, Matthew just keeps on rolling on the tile across the hallway somehow. I look down. Is that... Butter? Matthew finally reaches the other end of the slippery tile hallway and hits the wall. There was butter smeared everywhere.

"WHERE'S THE DOG?!" Matthew shouted so loudly I think it might have broken a window.

"There is no dog, Matthew James Harper!" I yell. Matthew continued to howl.

"Matthew! Did you actually believe our liars-of-sisters?" By this time, Matthew was roaring so loudly I'm not even sure he heard me. *It may be time to just dump this dork*, I think. Mindy and Aaliyah rolled on the floor, away from the smeared butter, laughing and pointing and screaming. Unexpectedly, Mrs. Harper walked in through the garage door. I guess she finished running her errands early.

She came running upstairs to investigate the screaming. She slips on the butter. How clumsy! Bad day for her, too. Then, a peach colored high heel slingshots, zipping across the hallway, past my too-shocked-to-move head. She thuds onto the tile floor. Matthew is still screaming. Aaliyah is singing Mickey Mouse Clubhouse. Their dad, I believe, is downstairs on the couch sleeping through it. *This family.*

Camille

I am about two and a half hours away from home when the worst thing possible happens. All of a sudden, my car starts making a weird noise and then just starts getting all bumpy, almost as if I was on a rocky road, but I wasn't. Then, it just drops, and a bunch of steam rises from my front bumper. After driving for twelve hours, I think I killed the car. *Good going, Cami.* And it being ninety degrees in Arizona probably didn't contribute to it either. I checked on my phone where the nearest town was. The nearest town was the city of Las Vegas. The one I was driving to. The one that was two and a half hours away.

There was only enough service to make one emergency call, but it was hard to decide who I should make the call to. Mom? Dad? Matthew? 911? Mom could track me and see where my phone is, so I figured that she would be the best option. I made the call.

Aaliyah

Okay. So, maybe I shouldn't have gone along with the plan. We got a huge ripping from Mom. Now me and Mindy had to spend the next hour cleaning it all up. If you've ever had to clean up melted butter, then you know how we felt. After taking Mindy and Delaney home, we got ready for bed.

In the morning, Mom and Dad didn't leave for work.

"Kids, we need to leave immediately. Camille's car broke down when she was driving from the airport. She missed her flight and is now stranded in the desert."

We loaded ourselves into the car and then left the house. It was going to be a long, hot, boring drive. But after maybe a half hour of driving, something interesting did happen. It wasn't a very good type of interesting, though. So, we got a call from the next door neighbor. They didn't have good news.

MATTHEW

We stopped the car. Mom stepped outside to talk. It was a million degrees. She was practically going ballistic by the time she hung up.

"Our house . . . has just been robbed. It was broken into, and one of the neighbors called the police. We need to go." All of a sudden the temperature increased, becoming even hotter than it already was. Okay, so our house has just been robbed, Cami is stranded out in the middle of nowhere, it's a billion degrees, there is no service or anything out here, Aaliyah is bored and needs another distraction, and we need to make the decision of continuing to Cami's location or going back home.

Mom and Dad started debating on what we should do. Do we leave Camille behind? Who knows how long it will take to reach her after this, though. Or do we let the robber get away? It was a tough decision. Eventually, we agreed that we needed to go back to see what was happening and be there with the police. We were much closer to home then to Cami. It would be miserable for her, but Cami would be okay. She just needed to stay put and wait a little bit longer. Aaliyah let curiosity get the best of her. She was asking questions and climbing the seats. I didn't say a word. My forehead was covered in sweat. I ached with fear.

Camille

I wait. What is taking them so long? It's not like there is any traffic out here in the middle of nowhere! Sweat drizzled down my cheeks, chest, and legs and hit the floor. What is taking them so long? My car was still smoking. I bet you anything I could fry an egg on the rocks. Then I'd eat it, because the last thing I ate was breakfast that morning and a bag of peanuts back at the airport. What is taking them so long? I try calling Mom, then Dad, then Matthew. No service. I take off my shirt to ring out the gallon of sweat absorbing into the fabric. I chug water from my water bottle that used to have ice in it. Now it was boiling. Thirsty, I try to scrape open a cactus. I was so desperate. You can guess how that ended. Thorns penetrated through my hand. I was dizzy and nauseous. I cough sickly, my heart thumping loud enough to be heard from miles away. I check the thermometer. 109 degrees. The air conditioner isn't working anymore. My own body feels like luggage. What is taking them so long? I lean against the steaming hot metal of the car door, trying not to collapse, but it doesn't work. I fall over onto the burning, rocky sand.

And everything goes black.

Aaliyah

When we finally arrive at the house, we see police cars pulled up on the driveway with cops and a guy standing next to them in handcuffs. There are bags full of our stuff thrown everywhere. I creep a little closer. Dad tells me to stay back. Instead, *he* goes up to the scene and asks for details, explaining how we live there. The police look back at us and motion to go with the neighbor back into their house.

Mrs. Norton gets us some warm, gooey cookies and a glass of cold milk. As we are eating, she starts telling us what she knows.

"I was the one who called the police. This man took a hammer and broke a window that led to the living room and then stepped inside. I pulled out my phone and immediately made the call. By the time they arrived his bags were full of your family's belongings, and he was getting into his car. Thank goodness they caught him."

All I could say was, "Whoa." Mom and Matthew thank her. I can't wait to go to school tomorrow and tell everyone about this. That was so dope! I wonder how Camille is doing. We still need to go pick her up.

7

Back with the Fam

MATTHEW

When the entire burglar thing was cleared up, we left to get Cami. It was a long, two hour drive. Aaliyah brought so many toys I had to sit in the very back, because there wasn't enough room for me.

We finally were able to track Cami down. I got out of the car and found her laying there on the wet sand. It was raining and super cold. She was a mess. Cami was covered in rainwater and little grains of sand, her makeup smearing her eyes. She looked relaxed, though. I picked her up and brought her inside the car. This definitely wasn't the way I would've liked to have greeted her, but at least she was safe.

We had enough service to make a call, so we called a tow truck to come and pick up her car. I had enough common sense to pack a towel along with us. I wrapped Cami in it and we started driving again. I woke her up.

"What took you guys so long?" Cami screamed. "I almost died." We explained the whole thing, and Mom and Dad apologized sincerely. The tow truck showed up. They loaded Cami's car in, and we took out her luggage. She fell asleep again, and crazy Aaliyah was playing so loudly it woke her back up. We drove back to the house and properly said hello, but Cami wasn't acting normal.

Aaliyah

I think the guy who decided to rob our house was taken to jail. It was kinda scary, I guess, but neat. We got our belongings back. I never thought we would actually be in a situation like that. That stuff only happens on the news. Well, that's what I thought up until today.

It is Downtown Las Vegas, though.

We picked up Camille. She seemed really annoyed with all of us. So I decided to have some fun and annoy her even more!

Camille

"Cami," I heard my name. It sounded like Matthew. I opened my eyes to see a bright light right above me. I was in a moving car covered by a towel.

"Hi Cami. It's us. You're a wreck," I heard Matthew's voice beside me. I opened my eyes. It was nighttime, and I was in a car with my family.

"Hi Matthew," I say. "I wish you guys had shown up sooner." I was in the very back of the car with him. Mom and Dad were in the front. And Aaliyah, who'd brought her entire toy box, was in her booster seat. There were so many toys she brought there wasn't even enough room for me to fit up there in the seat next to her.

"Where's my stuff?" I asked.

"Your suitcase is in here, and your car is getting towed." It was a long drive home. I was in a bad mood.

What Matthew warned me about with Aaliyah was absolutely right. She was really getting on my nerves. It seems like she gets worse every year.

"Hi Camille. Hi Camille. Hi Camille. You're back with the fam! Why do fish swim? Could a Polar Bear survive a day in Egypt? Have you ever realized that the only part of your reflection you can lick is your tongue? Hi Camille." That's what I listened to the entire two hours of driving back home.

"You are so patient, Camille," Dad said to me. Yeah, right I was patient. I was trying so hard not to scream. Matthew, on the other hand, wasn't.

"DO YOU EVER JUST SHUT UP?!" He yelled at Aaliyah. She started laughing. *You're trying to get on my nerves on purpose, aren't you?* I could tell that Aaliyah is the bad kid at school.

"Matthew!" Mom scolded him. "Be nice to the baby!" *Doesn't look like she's changed much, either. Bummer.* Dad had on a blank look. It was like he was asleep with his eyes open. That's the way he's been forever.

Aaliyah . . . has a tough personality, not gonna lie. Always has, and I feel like she always will.

My wish still hasn't come true. They haven't changed.

8

Aaliyah's Little Sidekick

MATTHEW

Today is the second to last day of school. It is also the end of the year dance. You want to know what else it is? That party. The one that we are throwing for Aaliyah, that me and Delaney have to volunteer at.

We walk down the block to her classroom. I didn't drive Aaliyah to school with me today. Instead, Mom did a little bit late. We want it to be a surprise. This is her first day back since the accident. It's not like she missed anything important.

Everything was set up. The tables, food, cake, and drinks. Mrs. Greyson, the teacher, had even started recording to see her reaction. We turn off the lights and get into hiding places as we see Aaliyah outside, getting her schoolwork and putting her backpack on the rack. She stumbles to the door on her crutches. As Aaliyah walks in, she stops. A little bit of light from the window is beating down into the room onto the banner that said "Get Well Soon, Aaliyah!" She must have seen it, because she looked around and said,

"Huh? Where are you guys hiding?" We all jump out at her, maybe a little too aggressively.

Aaliyah

Today when I got to school, I had to go to the office to get a tardy slip. Oh for crying out loud! It's almost the last day of school! Mom wasn't in a rush to get out of the house like usual. She was acting super weird. What's new, though? Matthew didn't drive me with him. I went with Mom. Something's up.

When I walk into the classroom, the lights are turned out. Then, the lights turn on. The entire class, including Matthew, Delaney, and my teacher Mrs. Greyson, jumped out at me, screaming the way Matthew does when we encounter a dog. It scared me so bad I forgot my crutches and just started running. The running didn't last for long. I stumbled over, hit a cheap, green, plastic table covered with pizza, fruit, a pitcher of fruit punch, and worst of all, a cake.

All of it fell over, including me. I think my cast might have cracked through the table.

The next thing I know, I am covered from head to cast in all of the above. My hair was slopped with cake. My limbs were sticky with fruit punch. Pizza was smeared across my brand-new froggy t-shirt and white jeans. Everybody was dying with laughter (especially Matthew) and pointing their fingers at me. Come to find out, Mrs. Greyson had been recording all of it. I lick some frosting from my lips.

All I could do was just go with it and laugh along with them, which is always the best thing to do in a situation like this, but on the inside, I was humiliated. *A simple* 'surprise' *would have been nice,* I think to myself over the roars of laughter. Ugh.

MATTHEW

Wow, that was awesome! I really hope Mrs. Greyson saved the recording, because I would love to put that on one of those funny fail shows. Mom was called over to the school to take Aaliyah home. She was a total wreck. It was incredible! I have no idea how they plan on getting that enormous thing of cake out of her hair. Best of all, that purple cast was just sopping with food and juice all the way through. That is going to be a problem.

The janitor needed to come in with a HACKSAW to cut the tiny green baby table out of her foot! It was the funniest thing I'd ever seen!

After school, I went home and got ready for the dance. I was so excited I could hardly wait. In just an hour from now, I would leave with Delaney, who is coming back home from school with me (but of course her little sister Mindy needs to come along as well), and we would go to the dance. Worriless. No Aaliyah. No Mindy. No dogs. No trouble.

It was just as we arrived at the school when I realized I spoke a little too soon.

Aaliyah

At home, me and Mom spent two hours getting all of that stupid gunk out of my hair. It was everywhere! I even had to throw my brand new outfit away! Mom then decided to take me over to the doctor to see what we should do about my cast.

When Dr. Dovalyn called me back, he took off my demonetized cast that was on me now for two and a half weeks and decided to do an X-ray before putting a new one on. We waited for a while in the room. When Dr. Dovalyn and the nurse came back into the room, they gave me news I had been waiting for, for a long while now.

My day turned from shattered windows to shiny diamonds.

Delaney

That party was a catastrophe. I went over to their house after school today with Mindy and got an update on Aaliyah. She wasn't wearing a cast! Instead, on her, there was a big black boot. It was bulky and had to be annoying the heck out of her, but at least Aaliyah could take it off when she wanted to.

"I still need to use these crutches sometimes," Aaliyah explained to everyone like she'd just won the Nobel Peace Prize. "But I will be able to go to Hawaii in August and can ice it freely. This will be easier." Matthew and I exchange looks. Camille, the big sister, was sitting right there as well. We communicated almost telepathically. *Oh yeah . . . the trip.*

Aaliyah

I am a little worried about this trip. I don't know why, though. I figured I needed to get my mind off of things for a little while. And I know just how.

I turn to Mindy. We need to do something to our siblings. I know just what.

"Come with me up to my room," I say. Mindy nods and helps me up the stairs. I explain the wicked plan to my naughty, beloved little sidekick. Mindy grins and agrees.

Mindy

We gotta move fast! Sure of it! The only hard part is waiting in the trunk of the car for however long it takes for those rotten teenagers to get ready and then not get caught until taking action! I'm not too worried about that, though, because Aaliyah and I have been doing this type of stuff our whole lives. We're very experienced.

Aaliyah

Me and Mindy load ourselves into the trunk and cover up with the towels Matthew left in there from his workout. Blech! Repulsive! But we need to do it in order to keep this plan going.

Mindy looks at her watch. 4:57. They should be coming out here any minute now.

Mindy

It's 5:01. The garage door opens. Matthew steps in the driver's seat. Delaney then gets in on the front passenger seat. Aaliyah giggles quietly. I shush her but smile. I can't believe we are actually doing this!

Aaliyah

The dented car pulls out of the driveway. Within minutes, we were in the high school parking lot. I look down the block at the elementary school. The light to Mrs. Greyson's classroom is on. *Probably cleaning up that disaster from today,* I think. A little stab of guilt hits me as Matthew and Delaney step out of the car. *What if they see us through the windows?!* I could tell Mindy was thinking the same thing. I shake my head. The windows are tinted, and we are smart and sneaky. We wait until Matthew and Delaney make their way into the gym. Then we step out of the car a minute later and start silently walking towards the gym.

You can do this.

9

Dance Disaster

MATTHeW

The gym is packed with music, people, and fun. So many activities! You'd never even be able to tell it was a gym!

"What do you want to do first?" I ask Delaney. "Why don't we get some food to eat before dancing? I haven't eaten since breakfast because of the whole 'get well soon party fiasco.'" We make our way over to the food and, while Delaney gets a plate of fruit salad, I stuff my face with ice cream and M&M's. Everything is going perfect until the entire party stops. The music no longer plays. Nobody is dancing anymore. All the voices stop except for two.

Aaliyah

We make our way up onto the big stage decorated in LED lights, balloons, and a DJ booth. Mindy creeps up to the DJ and asks for the microphone.

"Excuse me, me and my friend here need to make an announcement. We were told by Principal Reedy to be hired as announcement tellers or whatever here. Our siblings, Delaney Emerson and Matthew Harper, are nasty boyfriend-girlfriend and are standing over at the food table." The DJ totally believed us (typical teenager-brain thing) and stepped out of the way, stopping the music and handing the microphone to Mindy.

"Here, you have it after her," he said. Mindy starts up the plan we have been waiting for our entire lives.

Mindy

"Delaney Joy Emerson, I came in to tell you that your mommy has arrived to give you your daily diaper changing." Delaney whips around. I hear roars of teenage laughter. Ew! Gross! I could smell their bad breath! Now it was Aaliyah's turn.

"Matthew James Harper, for your information, you left your pacifier in the car where your stroller is." By then, nobody could take it any longer. The entire party, including the DJ, almost died laughing! Matthew and Delaney screamed and came running after us, box jumping onto the stage, tackling us, popping balloons, ripping down all of the decorations and Christmas lights, and then putting us in headlocks while punching.

"Aaliyah?!" Matthew yelled.

"That's my name!" She gave it right back to him. Delaney hit me ten times in a row. Teenagers are weak, though. Easily, Aaliyah and I fought back at them. It was almost like they were having some sort of psychotic breakdown or something! My life just got 1,000 times better!

Aaliyah

When Matthew tackled me, I was smart and used my humongous boot to kick him in the face. The entire place was a pigsty. Principal Reedy came in and ended it all. That dance was definitely going to be an important event in American History!

10

Camille's Homecoming

Camille

I was super angry at my family. Something could seriously have happened to me! I understand that the house was robbed, but that was being taken care of by the police! I am way more important than the items. When arriving back at home, I took a long shower and rested. In the morning, I felt a lot better. I cannot believe I just graduated college!

When Aaliyah came home from that get-well party, she was even worse than I was. Neither of us talked to each other much. I mean, what would we even say? She took me to the room where we would be staying in unlike every other year when I would just sleep on the couch. Together. It was her room. Well, mine. Now it was hers. Before I left for college, Aaliyah shared a room with Matthew. I'm sure she doesn't remember it, though.

As I walked in, I couldn't even get past the feeling of it. Everything was so . . . so whimsical and soft. There were flowy white curtains streaming down from the Juliette balcony window. Little silver butterflies were embroidered into it. Matching fabric flowed down from the silver bed crown that hung above her lacy, ivory bed. A pastel pink velvet quilt covered the butterfly print sheets. The only hanging items on the fresh gray walls were real, high-end, high-quality paintings of ghostly ballerina shadows. To top it all off, a crystal chandelier hung from the ceiling over the dreamy bed. There were toys on the floor.

How different all of this was from mine. I wish this could've been what my room looked like. I closed my eyes and pictured it. Rockstar posters slapped onto the turquoise walls. An unmade bed with a hot pink blanket. A canvas painting with an orange peace sign I had made in my boring art class. A broken bookshelf that held not books but all of my one million scrunchies and random knick-knacks. I asked Mom every single day to buy me a new shelf! She said no. Even on my birthdays. My desk that was unorganized with old homework assignments, makeup, and week-old water bottles that had been shoved into my overflowing drawers and forgotten about. I was a hoarder, but I was a teenager at the time. I'm not like that anymore. Nobody in our family is really a slob, anyway.

I opened my eyes. Of course Aaliyah didn't know about that. She paid no attention to me, and I never even cared. She only knows this lovely, angelic space. The only times Aaliyah ever really came in here when it was still mine was when she'd toddle through the doorway and grab something. Then, she would start chewing on it! I thought it was so gross back then. I would rip off my headphones and go running to save my precious property. Then I'd trip over a pair of jeans and not make it in time.

Most of my memories of Aaliyah are of her as a baby and toddler. She sucked her thumbs. She slept. She grabbed at her bronze bangs that are still there, almost as if she was trying to yank them right out. Then she cried. Mom tried to potty train her when she was three. Nothing so spectacular about little kids. Then, when she was going into kindergarten I left for college.

Never saw much of her. I wonder if she has memories of me.

Aaliyah

Memories of Camille Harper. Where can I start? She was like Matthew, a teenager out to make everyone's life miserable. If I am going to be spending an entire summer with her in the same room (her old room is now mine, but she still gets to use it for the summer), then I need to give myself a little memory boost. I take out a notebook that I use for sketching and turn to a fresh sheet of paper. I grab my feather pen and begin to write:

-She spent too many hours of the week in her messy bedroom, which is now mine, texting and doing who knows what

-She did her bucket loads of homework

-She was constantly going back and forth to the mall with friends

-She took forever in the mornings to get ready because she needed to do her hair, makeup, and find the perfect ensemble

-She ignored the world around her, focusing on nothing but beauty and text messages

-Sometimes, she wouldn't even come down for dinner because she was still doing something in her room

-She made interesting faces at me, almost as if she was hiding something

-All of this happened when she was about Matthew's age, maybe even a little younger. She could have changed by now. I mean, Camille is twenty-one . . .

Now my brain power was starting to kick in! But as I said, that was a long time ago. Camille was a teenager who had lost brain cells back then, and now her brain cells are probably back to the way they were when she was my age. So maybe she is different. Smarter. Nicer. It is time to see how this summer goes and make new and improved memories.

Camille

Okay, new plan. If Aaliyah is a mystery to me, then I need to find other ways to think of her then just a slobbery baby that I used to make rude faces at. Instead, I am going to ask Mathew what she is now like just to get the big picture. Operation: Aaliyah Investigation.

"Come on! This is really no time for jokes! Just tell me something simple. What toys does she like to play with? Maybe we could play sometime. That will probably help," I try to ask. Matthew is being absolutely no help at all.

"She's annoying, mean, and a complete waste of time. What more of an answer do you want, Cami?" I just aggressively nod my head and then walk back to mine and Aaliyah's bedroom. Fail. So I'll just ask Aaliyah myself.

Aaliyah

I don't like the fact that Camille and I need to be in the same room for the summer. From what I can recall, she doesn't really love me. We're awkward. So, I am going to make Camille feel at home and give her her original bedroom back. I could just sleep on the couch downstairs.

I pull my butterfly sheets off of my bed and bring them down to the couch. Then, I made my actual bed ready for nighttime and told Camille to do what she wanted.

Camille said that was kind of me to do, and that any time I wanted my room back, I can have it. Then, she stopped me.

"Aaliyah," she said.

"That's my name!"

"What do you like to play? Games? Toys? You can say anything." I stopped for a moment. *Huh?*

"I like Barbies," I told her. "And gymnastics, even though I have been taking a break because of my foot. Why?" I look at Camille. She is smiling. She shrugs.

"Well, I was thinking we could play together before going on the trip. Should we do Barbies, maybe?" I watch her take a comb out of her purse and brush through her stringy orange hair. Camille looks a lot like Matthew. They are definitely siblings.

"Okay," I say. "Let's get out the dolls. Maybe we could play out on the grass." Her dark brown eyes meet mine.

11

Mindy the Misery

MATTHEW

That is it! Aaliyah and Mindy are going to burn in fires as soon as I get a chance. They embarrassed me in front of the whole school! I tell Dad, Mom, and Delaney's parents. Delaney was just as distraught as I was. Then I look outside my window and see the little brat playing toys with Cami. Delaney comes over with Mindy, and our two families have a meeting about what happened.

Aaliyah

Camille and I are having so much fun! Doing mini games, dress-up, and make-overs. We make up little conversations that the dolls are having together and laugh with glee.

For the first time in my life, I feel connected to my sister. I tell her I love her, and really mean it. And for the first time in my life, I call her Cami.

* * *

Our fun is ruined when Mindy, Delaney, and their parents show up at our home. At first, this is exciting. That's because I thought Mindy was coming over for a play date. Turns out, this was no play date.

Delaney

We sit down at a table. I swear I have smoke coming out of my ears. Mrs. Harper has made cookies, but I am too mad to eat. I give dreaded Mindy the evil eye. *You are the worst sister ever.* Mrs. Harper starts out with talking.

"Girls, you both have a lot of explaining to do." Matthew looks just as boiling furious as I am. Mindy and Aaliyah exchange looks.

"So . . . It was kind of like a -joke . . ." Mindy the Misery starts out. For some reason, it is our silence that talks louder than our words. Then, Mrs. Harper continues.

"Aaliyah, you are grounded for the whole summer. And the only reason you are going to Hawaii is because your ticket has already been purchased."

Aaliyah looks down ashamed of herself.

The trip.

12

Matthew's Graduation

MATTHEW

Today I graduate high school! I'm in a much better mood. There's a graduation ceremony being held at school. Aaliyah is coming though, and so is Mindy. Let's see how this goes.

Aaliyah

I have to go to Matthew's graduation ceremony today. Dad was getting annoyed with Mom, because he thought I should just stay home.

"Tammy, don't bring her. She'll do something to embarrass her brother. Plus, she will be bored just sitting there for hours. You know how Aaliyah is."

"No, Mike, I want to teach my daughter good judgement! She needs to go to the ceremony!" *Mommy, going to a graduation ceremony isn't going to help with my 'good judgement.'*

We pull up to the school and walk to the field. Families fill the risers. I see Matthew standing down at the stage along with all the other graduates. He looks so ugly! He's wearing a square hat and black wrap. He looks like a nun! I scream and wave at him. Matthew looks in the other direction, but I know he heard me.

MATTHEW

That little two-faced, Aaliyah, was being obnoxious! She was screaming and waving only to annoy me! I pretended not to hear her.

The ceremony began. All the graduates got into a line. The principal got up on stage and started making a speech.

Camille

Mom was on my last nerve at that ceremony. She didn't even look at Matthew when he was up on the stage getting his diploma and didn't listen to a word during the principal's speech. About one third of the time, she was on her phone. The rest of the time, she played with Aaliyah's hair and took pictures. Get this: not pictures of Matthew but pictures of AALIYAH! Mom just snapped away, taking photo after photo of poor Aaliyah, who didn't want to.

This might sound crazy, but Aaliyah was actually doing a good job. She just sat quietly, ate crackers, and actually watched Matthew and the others graduate. Mom was the problem. Her phone was glued to her hand, and she only cared about Aaliyah, who just wanted to be left alone!

"Let's get a selfie, Honeybun!" Mom screeched. She leaned into Aaliyah's personal bubble zone and took pictures using little filters, missing the biggest moment of her son's life! Someone next to us shushed her. Aaliyah's thick, dark eyebrows said it all; she was MAD.

"Mommy stop! I don't want to take pictures! Watch the ceremony already!" Dad, who was half asleep, was at least clapping after every kid when they received their diplomas and was watching when Matthew was called up to the stage to get his. I took out my yellow Instax camera and took pictures of my brother.

Wow, Tammy Harper. Aaliyah is always going to be here. Matthew won't for much longer, though. This is more important.

Aaliyah

I am so done with Mom! She totally missed Matthew and every other kid being called up to get their diplomas, because she wanted to take selfies with me. Because "the sun in the background was pretty" and would "look good on the internet feed." I was speechless. Appalled. *Facebook Moms. Ugh. I'll think you'll survive getting off your social media stuff for fifteen seconds while Matthew graduates.*

"OMG, what hashtags should we use? I was thinking, #BestFriends #GirlsDay, #PrettyDaughter, and #Sunshine. Oh, and I also got these new sunglasses. I should put #Sunglasses."

Eventually, the ceremony came to an end. Matthew came over to us and we congratulated him. Mindy and Delaney and their parents came to see us as well.

"Wanna trade mommies?" I jokingly ask Mindy.

"No thanks," she says. "Yours is too annoying."

Mike Harper

You may not be able to stand her during this chapter. If you need inspiration, just think of me. I've been living with her for almost 25 years. Stay strong, you've got this.

Two Months Later

* * *

13

The Special Golden Bag

MATTHEW

I wake up to Mom's ear-shattering voice. Today is the big day! The day I will arrive in paradise. The trip I will be side by side with a dolphin. The trip I will ride a jet ski. The only bad thing about it is that Aaliyah's foot was fully healed, so she will be in full action.

"Kids! Time to get up! We need to make our way to the airport!" Our family makes the beds, gets dressed, and we all eat a light breakfast of fruit salad and an egg.

Aaliyah comes down. She is dressed in a lacy white shirt covered up by overalls, her hair tied up in pigtails with a little ribbon.

"I'm so excited!" she shouts out. I noticed that she has been in a very joyful mood lately. "When will the taxi be here?"

"Pretty soon, Aaliyah," Mom tells her with a little pat on the head.

"Sit down on the porch," I say. Aaliyah sits and smiles. I take a photo. We wait a little longer for the taxi to arrive. Then finally . . . FINALLY . . . it does.

"Aaliyah, let's go!" Dad yells out. Aaliyah is busy smelling the flowers. What a freak. It is love/hate between us. One moment, I want to throw her off a cliff. Then the next, I want to run and catch her.

"That's my name, Daddy! That's my name!"

*Yeah, **Aaliyah**, we know that's your name.*

Aaliyah

Now this is exciting! My first real trip! I feel a lot better now that Cami and I love each other for real. When the taxi driver does finally arrive, we load in our luggage and set off for the airport. I am so happy. I make Cami a little drawing of us playing with Barbies, having so much fun, and, as a gift for Matthew to give to him on his eighteenth birthday, I stuff in the shirt and $50 arcade gift card I had gotten for him with Mom into a shimmery gold bag. I can't wait to give this stuff to them.

"Don't do any crazy little sister stuff," Matthew leans in and whispers to me. "Not at the airport. No BBLS adventures just yet!" I nod. With Matthew putting that thought in my head, it actually made me worried that something might happen.

We got to the airport and got out of the car. The airport was a complete zoo. People shoved, ran, screamed, and everybody was in a rush to get somewhere. We got past the line and started loading our luggage onto the conveyor belt, and our family started walking over to the coffee shop. I look back at that mesmerizing suitcase carousel and then notice something horrible. I had put more than just my suitcase on the conveyor belt. I also put the bag with Cami's card and Matthew's birthday present! I needed to get it. That little bag could be destroyed in there, and once that happens, I'd never be seeing those gifts again!

I look back and dash towards the machine bumping into people on the way. I give myself a little lift. Finally, I am able to get up onto it. I'm able to get the gifts in my arms, which was good, but I wasn't able to hop down in time. It takes me and the luggage along with it. I screamed for help and the employees came dashing over. They were too late.

MATTHEW

Everyone was looking frantically for the missing kid. One employee came running over to us and said, "Your daughter went through the conveyor belt! We must shut it down immediately." Security guards came over, and an announcement was made over the loudspeaker.

"Attention flyers, if you see a little girl wearing light blue overalls and pigtails tied in an indigo ribbon, know that she is a lost child who has been separated from her family and report her right away." Once again, the attention is on crazy Aaliyah. I thought I told her to stay modest! Our flight was getting close!

Camille

The entire airport was looking for Aaliyah, who there had been no sight of. A flight attendant shut the conveyor belt down after somebody reported her being taken inside by it. The attendants went inside the belt and started calling her name.

I started to get worried. Was Aaliyah okay? That was dangerous. Plus, we may miss our flight! (That could not happen again). One of the workers went inside to look for her.

"Do you see anything?" asked the attendant.

"No."

Aaliyah

It was actually pretty enjoyable in that suitcase merry-go-round. All of the slides, ramps, and cool vibrant suitcase colors were amusing. I was sitting on top of my Barbie suitcase holding the presents. There was a cool breeze in the air, cooling down the usual Nevada summer heat.

I laughed, thinking about the faces and noises people would make when I bumped into them. It feels so good to make people mad and get away with it.

Then, all of a sudden, the ride stopped. Everything came to a complete stop. I thought I heard somebody calling my name but wasn't sure.

"Hello? Is somebody there? Can someone get me out of here?" There was no response. Then, a flight attendant came in and motioned for me to come with him and get out of there. We crawled through the machinery and exited the machine (ride, as I thought of it).

MATTHEW

Aaliyah had still not been found, and takeoff was in five minutes! People loaded their bags onto the plane and got in their seats. I could see Aaliyah's suitcase come out of the conveyor belt. On the other side, a flight attendant and Aaliyah herself come out! We went over to her and ran. Then, dumbest decision ever, we leave Aaliyah sitting on the bench alone while we went back to pick up our suitcase.

Aaliyah

When the others went to the conveyor belt to get our luggage, a kind looking woman pushing a stroller came up to me and sweetly said,

"Honey, the front desk needs you. They'll help you find your family." Oh boy. Everyone was looking for me.

"Oh, actually, they're just getting their suitcases. I'm okay." But then, the pilot said that I am too young to be waiting there alone and needed to come with him.

The pilot took me to the front desk and sat me down. My stomach turned. *Danget. I am in deep trouble.*

"Would the parent or guardian of Aaliyah Harper please come to the front desk? We have your kid." There were four minutes left before takeoff.

MATTHEW

Mom and Dad sent me to go get Aaliyah. I bumped into many people along the way. I felt bad when it happened; bumping into people is so rude. Finally, I got Aaliyah and we boarded the plane. Aaliyah sat down next to Cami and the plane started flying. I closed my eyes.

When I awoke, we were in Maui.

14

Oh Brother... And Sister!

Aaliyah

I gently took Matthew's phone from his pocket while he was asleep and held it up to his face. Effortlessly, the face ID worked and the phone unlocked. I downloaded 109 games (I counted twice) and played them for nearly the whole flight.

We got to Maui and Matthew awoke to the jerk of the plane. Time for vacay! That is when I decided to play a prank on Matthew.

I slid his phone out of its case. Then, as Matthew reached up to grab his suitcase from the top, I slid the case into his butt pocket where he normally keeps it. So good! I put his actual phone in my suitcase. Then we stepped out of the plane. The sun hit my wintery skin. Time for some sun!

Camille

We checked into the hotel and went up to our room. Our suitcases had been put in a golf cart to be brought up to us. It is on the top floor of the 4 story building. When I look out the window, I see a big pool with little islands on it. A few yards away from that, there was the vast, blue ocean. I saw Aaliyah stuff a shiny gold bag into her suitcase before the golf cart took them and drove away. When I asked her what it was, she just giggled and told me I would see later.

After a while, our bags had still not been delivered to our room. We went and told the front desk about it, and the lady said they had already been delivered to our room. *That is a little confusing,* I thought. After discussing it for a little while longer, we came to the conclusion that the cart had been delivered to the wrong room in a different building.

Aaliyah

I was guilty. Very, very guilty. Camille's drawing! Matthew's present! Worst of all, Matthew's stolen-by-me phone! All of it was in my suitcase along with my clothing and bathing suits. My suitcase didn't have a lock on it. Who knows what those people could do. I needed to get my suitcase back before Matthew found out that his phone was missing. Before those gifts were gone forever. Before this trip goes completely downhill.

MATTHEW

"I'm going to just go into the bathroom and put my swimsuit on while you guys go get the luggage back," I say. Mom and Dad are going to go over to the other room and get our stuff back. After that, we were planning on taking a dip in the spa downstairs. Mom and Dad left the room. Aaliyah, who is naturally pale, looked a lot paler. She was a total ghost. Her cheeks had a red tint. She started to sweat and fidget with her fingers and hair.

"I . . . actually need to go to the bathroom, too. There is one out in the hallway. I could just use that. Cami, you could go after Matthew. Matthew, take your time." Aaliyah dashes out the door. I figured she probably needed to poop or something because she already put her swimsuit on, but she was acting really weird—not to mention guilty. Something's up.

Aaliyah

I race to the elevator and zoom to the bottom. I needed to find my suitcase! I look at the map to find room B3, the room our luggage had been dropped off at. Matthew was about to realize his phone was missing. Mom will be furious if she finds out that I lost that present, even if it was the golf cart driver's fault.

As I creep around the corner of the wall, I see room B3. Mom and Dad knock on the door and a little kid who had to have been no more than three or four opens the door. Oh for Pete's sake! Just give us our belongings! As I sneak up a little closer, I notice something terrifying. That girl was wearing an oversized *Hurley* shirt. In her hand was a crumpled sheet of paper that had a drawing of two girls playing with dolls on it. And on top of that drawing were scribbles drawn in orange marker. Noooooo!!!! For some reason, that girl looked very familiar to me.

15

Sibling Suspicions

Camille

"Uhhh, Cami? Are Mom and Dad back yet?" Matthew calls to me from inside the bathroom.

"Oh, uh, no. It's only been a few minutes. Why?" There was a pause. Then Matthew spoke up again. Only this time, he sounded kind of angry.

"Is Aaliyah back yet?!" She actually wasn't back. I said no.

"Okay. Tell me when she's back."

MATTHEW

I slipped off my shorts. Out falls a phone case. Confused, I put on my bathing suit. I stay in the bathroom and look for my phone. About ten more minutes pass and I call out to Cami. Aaliyah once again has struck.

Aaliyah

"Sweetie, are your parents here?" Mom asks the little girl. *Hurry up!* The little kid just slams the door on Mom and screams out to her mother. A pretty black-haired lady steps out and apologizes for her kid's behavior. The three of them go further out into the hallway and start talking. I make a run for it, sneaking into the room while their backs were turned. There, lying on the carpet, was what I was looking for. It just wasn't in the best condition.

MATTHEW

"Aaliyah! Aaliyah, are you in there?" I screamed and pounded on the bathroom door. There was no response. All of a sudden, I no longer felt so angry. I was actually starting to become worried. From what it seemed, Aaliyah was actually not in there. It didn't even feel like the door had been locked!

"Aaliyah, I'm coming in if you don't respond to me right now!" There was still no answer. People were beginning to poke their heads out of their doors. I was seriously nervous now. Just as I had said, I turned the knob and opened the door to the restroom. Cami and I stepped inside.

Delaney

I wonder how Matthew is doing. I should probably call him to check in. So I pick up my phone and dial his number. After it rang a few times, I heard Aaliyah's voice. It was more high-pitched than normal and very quiet in the background.

"Hewwwwwo?" Aaliyah asked.

"Hi Aaliyah, this is Delaney. How are you guys doing? Would you mind giving the phone to Matthew?" Aaliyah continued being weird.

"Can I have a teddy-weddy bear with a sticker book?" Okay. Now it was just Matthew being an idiot. Why haven't I dumped him yet?

"Matthew, come on," I lecture. Matthew said some more random comments, and I hung up. Right before, I heard a loud crashing noise.

Aaliyah

I don't think that little girl saw me run inside. While she was busy scribbling all over Cami's card, I curled up under the bed. Then, there was a noise coming from inside my suitcase which was sprawled out on the carpet. The cell phone screen lights up and I see Delaney's number. Great. *Delaney, this is not a good time.* The girl answers. Oh no oh no oh no oh no.

"Are you my Daddy?" She shouts into the speaker. Delaney probably thought she was me! Then, just before Delaney hangs up, the kid throws it across the room. I scoot a little closer and try to reach for the phone and some items from inside my suitcase.

Mom, Dad, and the kid's mom walked in. I had to just stay under the bed. They couldn't find out I was in there. They would be so mad. They took our suitcases.

"Thanks! Have a good trip! Do you guys have everything?" *Absolutely not,* I think. Mom and Dad walk out of the room and the door closes. I was still under the bed, holding a bunch of stuff and sitting in a swimsuit!

"What is all of this?" The woman says and picks up the items I was holding.

"Don't know," the girl says. Why does she look so familiar? Her Mom runs out of the room up to my parents and asks them if those clothes and Matthew's cell phone belong to us. Of course, they only take one of my shirts! Uggggggggg! Plan B: when these people leave their room, I will grab the rest of my belongings and make my escape.

Problems with Plan B: who knows how long it may be until they leave their room.

Camille

As Matthew and I open the door to the bathroom, it is just as we expected. Nobody was in there. I guess it's time to go on another Aaliyah search.

MATTHEW

7:42 P.M. My insane little sister is still missing. What is wrong with her? Everywhere we go, something needs to happen! Now it is getting old and a little embarrassing.

16

Actions Have Consequences

Aaliyah

I swear, I am really getting good at hiding and waiting. I watched the clock hour after hour while I waited under that tight, dusty bed and listened to the kid scream and babble and yank at her hair. It never stopped. She definitely reminded me of somebody. After a little while, I almost just laughed really hard at how dumb all of her moods were. I thought about it, and then I knew who it was. I knew who she resembled, just a younger version.

Me. Reddish-brown hair. A perfect line of her shiny, thick bangs. Crystal blue eyes that were close to some tiny freckles.

I've seen so many pictures of myself from her age and heard funny stories about the things I'd done back then.

A little bit on the wild side but can still give you a good laugh. I could feel Matthew, all of a sudden. When I stepped through that door, when I first got a glimpse of her. I thought she was crazy. Annoying. Little and immature. I'd honestly never felt that before. Now that I have, my vision of Matthew has sort of changed from the one I have had my entire eight years of life. Anyway, though, I believe that the world revolves around me so I will be as mean and annoying as I want towards Matthew, because it feels good.

You'll not believe me when I tell you exactly how long I was under that bed. It was three whole hours at the least. I could only imagine my parents right now . . . Mom shrilling like a possessed chicken and Dad half asleep. I made sure to stay quiet and covered by the bed skirt.

Those were some of the hardest hours of my life. I had to remain quiet, even though it was SO hot and SO dusty. That girl was SO loud, and she continued to destroy my stuff when her mom left her to take a shower, unattended! It's official; I hate babies. I really hope I never have one when I'm a grown-up.

I began to realize that, even though my prank gave me a good laugh in the beginning, I've now ended up having to pay for it. It's true what they say; actions do have consequences.

MATTHEW

"That's it," Mom said. "I'm calling the police." It has been hours since Aaliyah was last seen.

"Mhm," Dad mumbled. I don't think he was too worried. Because really, Aaliyah going missing is just a part of our daily lives at this point. Give it a little while, and she'll be back! Mom doesn't understand that, though. She's . . . a little bit on the crazy side.

Camille

"When was the last time she was seen?" the police officer asked us. I was sitting on a cold metal chair at the police station.

"A few hours ago," Matthew says. *How much longer until we get to just leave?* I look at my watch. We have been in this "top secret involved people only" room for almost an hour, maybe a little less, but it feels like forever. I toy with my hair. I bite my nails and cuticles. I try to play a game inside my head to pass the time. Mom is worried sick. Dad is half asleep. Aaliyah is still missing. I do have to say she's been gone for quite some time, but even then, just why are we here? Why has this become an investigation? This mischief has been going on for eight and a half years now, and Aaliyah will always come back on her own. Everything always ends up being okay.

It has actually been several hours now since Aaliyah went missing, though.

Aaliyah

It was getting late out. It was almost dark. When finally . . . just finally . . . the people get hungry and leave the room for dinner.

I crawl out from under the bed, collect my stuff, and run out to find my family. I go back up to our room and knock on the door for them to unlock it and let me in. Nobody comes to the door, though. I didn't have a key, of course, so there was really nothing that could be done. WHERE IN THE NAME OF GOD WERE THEY?! WHAT ARE THEY DOING THIS LATE WITHOUT ME?! Well, I guess my only option at this point was to just sit here and wait for them to come back.

I sit by the door and wait. My patience is seriously improving. That's when I hear an ugly, too-familiar voice and see an ugly, too-familiar face.

MATTHEW

The police came with us back to the hotel. We needed to search the entire place. I was helping search. We looked everywhere. In laundry rooms, in different hallways, in the lobby. That's when I started thinking outside the box.

"You guys," I told our crew of Mom, Dad, Cami, and a security guard. "Let's go check up in our room. Maybe Aaliyah decided to go back and is waiting for us to unlock the door!"

Turns out, I was right. I went running down the hall. Aaliyah, still in her sparkly pink bikini, was sitting on the carpet waiting for us to unlock the door.

"The Baby!" Mom screamed. She is really getting on my nerves. We thanked the security guards and police as they left.

Aaliyah explained everything. How she took my phone, stayed in that room the whole time, and much more. When I opened up my phone, there were rows and rows of games waiting to be discovered. Repulsive Aaliyah. The battle is on! Oh, it is so on!

Aaliyah

I stared at Cami's fiery orange hair. It glared at me, crimson red. I was just so guilty!

Mom was giving me hugs and kisses and telling me she was so glad I was back. I winced and tried to pry her off of me. Dad was annoyed and asleep at the same time. We were having a talk.

"We were truly scared, Aaliyah," Dad started. "You are so irresponsible. For now, I'm just going to forget about it. So say you are sorry to us and let's move on with this trip. Next time, nobody is going to be as nice."

Wow, Dad spoke! A lot!

17

Tether Trouble

MATTHEW

As an activity for my birthday, rock climbing is coming up next. I really think it is time for Mom and Dad to lecture Aaliyah a little harder. She is never going to improve if everybody is always letting her bad behavior slide.

The next night, a taxi shows up and brings us to the rock wall. It's nighttime, and the sky is dark, but with all the lights and bonfires on the beach, it's bright.

When we arrive, I tell Aaliyah to just do as the people say and not make up any "Aaliyah Rules" that would cause trouble, not that my words were even going to do anything. Aaliyah nods.

When we got to the wall, each of us got a helper that gave us our harnesses and kept us safe during climbing. I paid close attention to each. There was one really pretty girl who looked about my age. Oooh. Then there was a wrinkly old lady. *Yow.* I decided to call her Mizz Wrinkles. Pretty Girl is still my #1 choice. The third person was a fat middle aged lady who looked bored and like she didn't want to be there. I was not really a big fan of Fatso either. The fourth was a guy maybe in his twenties who wore big, black framed glasses and an oversized shirt. Bigshirt seemed friendly, but Pretty Girl was still in first place. And finally, there was a dude who seemed very concerned about his job. He wore a professional name tag and clothes, and he checked everyone multiple times to make sure we were all safe. I thought that could be a good sign. Then, I saw him asking the manager if he could have extra money since he cared so much about safety. *Pfffft.* I called him Cheesy Employee.

They chose us each one by one. Poor Dad ended up with Mizz Wrinkles, the old lady. Then, Bigshirt went to Cami. Cheesy Employee went over to Mom and said that he was going to make sure this was a safe and enjoyable trip for the whole family.

My crazy mom said, "Oh yes! Be sure that my little baby Aaliyah has a great time, the best of her young life!" Yugh. They are perfect for each other.

Up next, it was Pretty Girl's turn. I crossed my fingers and my toes. Finally, she was walking over toward me with a gentle smile. Yes! Yes! Yes! Right as I smiled back, Pretty

Girl kept on walking without even looking at me. Not even once.

"Awwww! Hi cutie! I love your little pigtails! What is your name?" Pigtails? I don't remember putting my hair in pigtails.

"Hi! My name is Aaliyah! I'm so excited!" Aaliyah said in a voice that was a lot squeakier than usual. What? No!!!! If Aaliyah got Pretty Girl, then that means . . . my rock wall companion is going to be Fatso.

Fatso came booming over to me and handed me a tiny harness.

"I think it's a little too small," I said. Fatso grunted and grabbed a bigger one. She threw it to me with a groan. *This is why you go to college. So that you don't end up like Fatso,* I told myself. I looked over at Aaliyah and Pretty Girl.

"Now, put this foot through here!" Pretty Girl said to Aaliyah. She made sure to get Aaliyah the cleanest, pinkest harness on the shelf. Aaliyah giggled and looked over at me. She widened her eyes, folded her hands into a heart shape, and made kissy lips.

Pretty Girl lifts Aaliyah up into the air and says, "I think this harness is perfect on you!" Then, she holds Aaliyah face to the ground and runs, making zooming noises like an airplane.

"Weeeeeeee!" Aaliyah shouts. Mom runs in with her camera and snaps 400 photos of Aaliyah being whizzed around by a stranger, acting like it's all cute or whatever.

Fatso tells me I am good to go, and I take my place on the sky-scraping rock wall.

The manager blows his whistle and we start climbing. I had a nice view of the ocean and town. Hawaii is incredible. I felt super relaxed, at first, but then that brother instinct inside of me said this wasn't going to end well.

Aaliyah

I started climbing up the rock wall. It was awesome, but we ran into a problem. I guess you can guess which kind. BBLS.

All of a sudden, my tether unattached. And I was in the middle of a rock wall! I screamed for Shawntae, the girl who was my climbing companion and Matthew's new crush (poor Delaney), to come up and help me.

"GO! GO! GO! WHAT IS GOING ON?! HELP HER!" Shawntae yells. I am holding on with all my might. Security guards came running through the gates. There are tweeting whistles, everyone is screaming, and I am hanging there silent. My arms are really starting to get tired!

MATTHEW

Aaliyah was hanging off. Now I am starting to wonder if hoping for Pretty Girl to help me with my harness was a bad idea. Aaliyah could seriously be in danger. Finally, she starts yelling out to me, of all people,

"Matthew! Help me!" Oh boy.

"Well what should I do?" The security guards continue blowing whistles and running after all of us. One guy even gets a ladder and starts climbing up. I can hear sirens. Someone had called the fire department.

"Matthew! Jump down! I could grab on you so you can help me!"

"No way am I doing that! I'm not getting killed on my birthday!" The sound of sirens, screaming, and whistles filled my ears. Aaliyah's screams are the loudest of all.

"HEEEELLLLLLLPPPPP MEEEE!!!!!" Aaliyah continued to shout. A firefighter started climbing, but they would be too late. Aaliyah was too tired to hang on longer.

Aaliyah

Finally, I see Matthew starting to lower down on his side of the wall. His side was right next to mine. So I wait for him to climb down, step by step. Finally, Matthew climbs low enough to my level. I notice that Mom and Dad are doing that as well, but Matthew was low enough. I brace myself and fall onto him, grabbing his tether.

"Aaliyah! What are you doing? What is going on?" The police continue to climb up, a little confused.

Matthew held me tight and carefully let go of the tether, and we fell to the bottom. We touched the floor and saw the others come down. After we all calmed down, we left and decided to eat dinner at a nearby restaurant. Surely no trouble could happen there . . .

18

Psychos on a Slide

Camille

Whew! What a night! All I can say is, Matthew was absolutely right about Aaliyah being psycho. Our night got crazier when we went out to dinner right after all that commotion.

"Aloha, my name is Dan. What may I get for you this evening?" the waiter asked us as we sat down at a fancy booth. It was behind curtains made of Hawaiian beads in a leather booth under a stringy chandelier. Tiki masks hung on the walls.

"Macaroni and cheesy weesy!" Aaliyah screamed loud enough for the entire country to hear. *Wow. How is Matthew able to live like this every single day?!*

A little while later, Aaliyah needed to use the restroom. Oh great. The second she walked out of the booth, she saw a playground from the window up ahead. Double oh great.

"Look, Mommy! Can I go to that playground?" Everybody exchanged looks. *How 'bout we just stick to using the restroom, Aaliyah . . .*

"Of course you may go! Matthew can take you! Right, bud?!" She nudged Matthew with her elbow. Oh great. Oh great. Oh great.

"Don't call me bud anymore! I am too old for it!" Matthew tells her. Poor Matthew is basically forced to take Aaliyah out to play on a green tube slide.

"We'll call you when dinner is here!!!" Mom says all cheerfully. Matthew stares daggers at us and walks out with the crazy eight-year-old sister.

Tammy Harper

I love my kids. It is so nice to see those sweetie pies getting along great! Especially my absolutely-perfect-never-can-be-any-better diamond child, Aaliyah Jasmine Harper II (she is named after ancient Alamiỹýáh Jaśmihhá Harpiéré I, my great great great great great great grandmother from France who lived around the 14th century), because she deserved something a little extra special.

My husband, Mike, really couldn't care less about my over-obsessive attractions toward my booshy-wooshy Aaliyah, but in my eyes, she could do no wrong, commit no crimes, and have no mishaps across her splendiferous journey through her marvelous life, other than some minor 'issues' going on every now and then. Because really, that little cutie-bajooty is only eight! And she doesn't get into BBLS troubles everywhere we go.

Now do not get me wrong; I love Camille Grace and Matthew James; they are just older now and know their lessons. Camille is named after another French woman we are related to called (get prepared, this is quite the long one!) Chham `allaalalahihaya ~amakahiya ^caliyah} vrindivaanliyah Gracieré Harpiéré XV. (Now you can see why I decided to simplify that Roman/French name down to Camille Grace). I only named her after Chham `allaalalahihaya ~amakahiya ^caliyah} vrindivaanliyah Gracieré Harpiéré XV because Mike told me to. I didn't care.

Last of all, Matthew James. I honestly didn't care when I named him. Neither did Mike. He was kind of over the whole kid thing at that point.

I look out the window and see a tourist banging on it, pleading for our help. Okay! I take it back! Perfect Aaliyah Jasmine Harper really does get into BBLS trouble everywhere we go! It's okay though, because she has a happy spirit and wild soul.

"Hello, your kids yelled to me to tell you they are stuck in the slide and need help," she hollered. She took a photo.

Oh, my! I will make sure my favorite daughter is okay! Ohhhhhhh my!!!!!

Aaliyah

I decided to play a prank. A prank that would scare the life out of Mom. So here's how it goes: I get in that tube slide and curl up into a ball to make it look like I'm stuck. I'll tell Matthew that I'm stuck and ask him to give me a shove. When he reaches inside, I'll grab him and pull him in to get HIM stuck then slide down afterward, leaving him behind! This was going to be so funny!

I lowered myself into the slide and bent my body. I shouted up to Matthew.

"Help me! I'm stuck in the middle of this thing!" So Matthew came racing up to get me. It was actually starting to get a little stuffy and claustrophobic in there, and I began to regret doing it. My feet were bent over my head, and my arms were in an awkward position. I had to stick it out, though. I wanted to accomplish my mission.

"Okay, fine. I'm coming, Aaliyah." Matthew sounded annoyed. I sit there for the next few minutes waiting for Matthew to climb the dumb ladder.

"I'm here!" Matthew yells, acting like he's purposely trying to leave me in longer and give me heart failure. I look up at the top of the spiral slide, but I don't see a face. All that's there are buttcheeks. I mean, he's a buttface, but that's not literal. So, Matthew is now barricading the exits! How unsatisfying!

"Just reach in and give me a shove so I can get to the bottom!" Matthew pushes with all his might to get into the slide himself and detach me.

"I'm . . . *gasp* trying . . . to . . ." he says dismissively. I roll my eyes.

"Oh for crying out loud, Matthew! Don't go down butt first. Go headfirst like a normal human being!" As if my question was ignored, he slid down butt first. Then he bumped right into me. I grabbed him by the waist and brought him in deeper. I tried to slide down, but with him on top of me, it was impossible! I was actually stuck in the slide! The plan sure wasn't working out the way I wanted it to!

"Great, you idiot, now we're both stuck." Matthew yells to a tourist to tell the others through the window that we needed help.

"Look for the blonde woman who is wearing sunglasses inside, sitting next to a sleeping man!" the woman yells up through the exit of the slide that she'll do what she can. I heard her camera start clicking.

After a few minutes of waiting, I heard Mom screaming, Dad snoring, and Cami muttering under her breath up from above.

"Help is on the way! We'll make a call to 911 to come and get you guys out of there!" A group of nosy tourists file into rows to watch and pull out their cell phones, taking photos like their life depended on it.

The smell of sewage fills up my nostrils to the max and almost suffocates me. The god-awful stench was multiplying. I could almost *hear* my poor, innocent lungs talking to me, begging for forgiveness. *Probably because Matthew's butt is an inch from my face,* I think. Of all people, it needs to be Matthew Harper. Literally. Of all people. I do know one thing, though! I will sleep well tonight after all that adventure! Or so I thought. Tomorrow was Matthew's birthday! I needed to wrap his present so he won't notice and draw Cami a new picture!

MATTHEW

I could hear the sirens of a fire truck pulling into the driveway. For the second time tonight. Aaliyah shrieks.

"Be quiet! My ear is right here!" I tell her. *She takes after her mother.* Yet still, nothing is louder than the clicks and snaps of cameras. Firemen climb up onto the big toy and try to lower themselves into the jam-packed slide. They are way too big, though. So they stop and have a discussion. Five minutes or so later, Dad shouts up to us saying that the only way to do this is to cut the slide off! I thought that was a bunch of baloney at first, but it turns out Dad was right. Above my head, I could hear the sound of drilling. *Whizzzzzz. Whirrrrr.* Unbelievable. Well that sure blows for the kids who *can* fit in there.

Eventually, the firefighters are able to take it off. Aaliyah cheers and whoops with joy. There are caution cones and tape closing off the "hazardous" area.

"Climb down!" the fireman tells us. I push Aaliyah off first. I heard more cameras clicking like paparazzi. This will be viral in ten minutes or less.

"Twit-a-roooo!" she screams like a one-year-old. Wow. Then I lower myself down. As I jump off and hit the floor, I see Aaliyah being talked to by the fire chief. She looks very guilty.

Jacen M. Katt, Fire Department Chief

I don't know how many more times this girl is going to get into trouble, but my department has been called twice in one night from these tourists, Mike and Tammy Harper. Each time we or the police department get a call, it's that Mommy Tammy trying to save her nutty daughter. I really don't know how much longer I or my workmates can take these people.

I start talking to the little one, Aaliyah. She's apparently eight, but I think she could pass for six. She's short and skinny and acts so immature. I really don't understand how she got stuck in that slide. She was definitely small enough to fit.

Her other two siblings, Camille and Matthew, are nothing like that. They aren't so hyper-active.

"Aaliyah, can you prove to me that you're too big for that slide? It's meant for kids your size and age. I don't see how you'd not be able to fit." She looks at me with a red face.

"I'm sorry. I must admit this, but it was a prank. I wasn't stuck. I was trying to get my brother stuck to be funny." How appalling. We were at work, we had more important things to do, and we just wasted our time helping this girl who had tricked us for laughs?! I explained to Aaliyah that things like this weren't funny, not when it gets to the point of a 911 call. There could have been someone who actually needed us.

Honestly, I think I am a better parent to that Aaliyah kid than her own parents.

Tammy Harper

That donkey, Jacen Katt, the head of the fire department, hurt The Baby's feelings! He put her to shame and had a talk about responsibility with her. She's just a baby! How come nobody notices that?

He said some brutal things right to The Baby's tiny, innocent, angelic face! How harsh, disrespectful, and rude! I will not let that slide for all The Baby is worth!

"Jacen, don't you ever talk to The Baby that way again! She is the most perfected creature to walk this Earth at the very moment! You have to realize that she is only eight! She is truly God's little angel! And mine!" Jacen just stares back at me. Aaliyah tries to tell me she's fine.

"No, seriously, it's fine, I'm okay."

No! It is not okay for somebody to talk to The Baby that way! I see Mike slap his head and a tourist snap a photo.

MIKE HARPER

I'd like to crawl under a rock to sleep and hide.

19

The Ice Cream Fiasco

Delaney

Matthew and I are very alike. So are our sisters. For example, today. Mom forced me to bring Mindy out to the new ice cream parlor across the street. She forced me to. Which meant I of course needed to.

"Let's go!" Mindy shouts. We walk into the parlor and order our treats when Mindy drops her water bottle and it spills everywhere. I clean it up with napkins and walk outside to throw them away. I sat out there for a bit. When I walked back inside to get her, I was speechless.

There was Mindy, holding an ice cream cone with ice cream on top of it. Not just a scoop of ice cream, though . . . there were stacks of scoop after scoop after scoop, piling up to the sky.

"Why did you let her get that?!" I tell that useless, teenage ice cream server. "She is nine." The girl looks back at me, embarrassed.

"Mindy, what were you thinking?" I tell her. "That is gonna be so, *so* expensive! You can't eat that!" Mindy's mouth breaks into a massive smile.

"So I could throw it at you, instead," is her answer. At first, I am a little confused. *At first.*

"Right here, and right now."

Mindy

Delaney was being a big jerk to me this morning. She was chucking food at me and calling me names while we were eating breakfast! So I formulated a plan. Mom had told Delaney that she needed to take me out to the new ice cream parlor across the street. When we get there, I'm going to make a mess for Delaney to have to clean up. When she walks outside to the trash can, I'll order. It will be a seven scoop with sprinkles and a cherry on top! Then, when Delaney walks back in, I will get my payback. I will chuck that entire thing of ice cream back at her and call her names just as she did to me this morning. It was going to be so funny!

Camille

That night, after all the commotion was over, I climbed up into my bunk hoping that I would fall asleep and everything would be over. I've been trying hard to forget this day happened. After all, it was Matthew's birthday vacation. In three days, we'd be going back home.

"Well, I suppose you may choose a souvenir as well, Camille." We were at the gift shop the next morning, and Aaliyah was deciding what she should get. Of course, her thing needed to be a stencil that spelled out *PUNCH ME.* Oh great. Just great.

"Mom, are you really going to let her get that? Just imagine the plan behind it . . ." I whisper to Mom.

"Anything for The Baby!" Mom says all joyfully and loudly. *Wow.*

I chose a relatable keychain that said *"eat, sleep, study, repeat."* Matthew was out on the beach sunbathing. Little did I know, BBLS problems were about to strike once again. Actually, I take it back. Not "little did I know," I feel like I knew quite a bit about this BBLS takedown and what would come of it.

Delaney

Less than a split second later, I was sopping head-to-toe in pink ice cream! Mindy the Misery is going to pay. I scream and run behind the counter where all the ice cream is served and scoop up with my hands an entire bucket of ice cream then put it over Mindy's black hair like a mask. She screams! The entire time all of this is happening, the server is sitting in the corner on her phone! Is she that oblivious she doesn't realize her store is turning into that school dance Mindy the Misery also ruined?!

Mindy, still with the ice cream over her head, runs over to the sprinkle shaker and dumps it out everywhere. The idiot finally notices what is happening and runs to get her boss. She basically just stole all that ice cream! A few seconds later, the boss dude comes out and . . .

Aaliyah

I felt a little bad and guilty about the whole slide thing. I thought of it more as a joke when I planned it out, and I didn't realize the fire department would be involved within minutes.

That night, I was planning out a new present for Matthew. I took a piece of paper and drew Cami a new card, then took the shirt that little girl ruined and washed it in the tub.

The next morning, Mom took me and Cami to the gift shop and let us buy a souvenir. It was really hard at first to choose between a beach Barbie and a chef Barbie, but then I saw a big stencil that said *punch me* on it. How random, but how perfect! Forget about the Barbies! Matthew was on the beach lying on his belly. I knew what I was going to do.

Mindy

"YOU GIRLS ARE IN SO MUCH TROUBLE!!!!!! JUST WAIT UNTIL YOUR DAD FINDS OUT ABOUT THIS!!!!! YOU . . ."

Aaliyah

I finished my shopping and walked down to the beach with Dad. I looked around for Matthew and walked over to him. I placed the *punch me* stencil gently on Matthew's back. The sun was going to burn through and make a tan line that said "Punch me," and then there will be no turning back! I did some gymnastics stunts on the beach to pass the time and waited for Matthew to wake up.

I didn't realize that I hadn't put on any sunscreen. Matthew wasn't the only one getting badly burned today.

20

& Burn

MATTHEW

I think I fell asleep there on the beach. When I woke up, I was ready to go back to the hotel. Aaliyah was out there swimming and doing gymnastics, and Dad was sitting in a sun chair on his phone. Aaliyah was as red as a lobster. *Well, that's what happens when you don't bother putting on sunscreen, dummy.* I stood up, and this weird stencil that had the words *Punch Me* on it seemed to have fallen from the sky. I just shook my head and ignored it.

Then, my phone buzzed. I picked it up to see the notification. *Instagram: Sara Garcia posted a photo and it's gone viral!* Huh? I don't know anyone named Sara

Garcia . . . I opened Instagram. There was a picture of me and Aaliyah stuck in the slide and the fireman sawing it down. The caption said: WHEN IDIOTS TRAVEL. Great. Now I'm a meme.

I saw Dad rubbing aloe vera gel on Aaliyah, who definitely didn't get along with the sun today, under an umbrella. Then, that little brat got up from the towels and punched me!

"Aaliyah! Apologize! We do not punch!" Dad yelled at her. Aaliyah laughed hard and said something a little suspicious.

"Well then why do you have letters on your back then spell out '*punch me*?'" That was a little confusing.

"Turn around," she said. Dad gasped. Aaliyah was practically dying with laughter. It seemed hard for her to catch her breath.

"I totally got you!"

Aaliyah

Matthew's reaction was different than mine, and so was Dad's. Nobody but me seemed amused with Matthew's sun tattoo.

When Cami and Mom got back, Mom said the usual answer.

"Just give her some grace, you guys! You need to understand that she is only eight! It really is not her fault! She doesn't understand that what she did was wrong!" I liked that I could get away with everything, but honestly, sometimes it got annoying and embarrassing. People started staring at us. One girl took a picture.

"You know what, Tammy?!" Dad finally exploded. Ooooh! Yes! I love watching people fight! Soak in all the juicy, steamy gossip! In case you haven't noticed, I live for heated conversation. And, I just learned what Dad actually sounded like!

"You are right!" he continues. "It isn't her fault! It is YOURS! YOUR fault Aaliyah is not improving when it comes to behavior! You let everything she does slide! That is BAD parenting! The biggest punishment she has ever gotten from you is probably the time she used up all that makeup at the mall and Matthew had to spend his money that was saved up for his dance suit! And, even then, all you did was yell for a little while! Time to grow up! Time to let her learn! If anything, I feel bad for Aaliyah because she will never learn at the rate you are going! It's time we teach her to stop with these pranks or whatever it is she's doing!"

Mom was shaken. Cami and Matthew were looking down at the sand and frowning. Many others who were on the beach started staring. A tourist took a photo. I thought about it for a little while. What Dad said *was* right. Mom never gets mad at me, even when I do get off-task. It was starting to get old. I didn't like it when Mom stood up for me to that poor firefighter. It was embarrassing and unfair to him. I'm not saying I like getting in trouble, because I don't. I just feel embarrassed when people stare and laugh and take pictures and make weird faces because of the things Mom says.

"Why are you telling me I have not been raising my child correctly?" Mom said angrily.

"Because it's true. You needed to know. She is no longer a baby; she needs to learn right from wrong," Dad said, lowering his voice a little. By now, Mom was livid.

"You know what?! I need some time to myself. Don't be surprised if I never come back to you abusive fools!" she spat dramatically. Okay . . .

Mike Harper

That was the most I've said since Aaliyah started walking.

Delaney

That was . . . interesting. Mom and Dad were furious at Mindy and I. A hunk of money had to be spent on that ice cream.

$285.97. *Wow.* That was going to be coming right out of our allowances. I should probably call Matthew and fill him in about this one. He is coming home in just three days! I have no idea how he is doing.

MATTHEW

"C'mon, kids," Dad told us after Mom's little scene. I swear there were tourists recording videos on their phones. Aaliyah was so sunburned that Dad was taking her to see a doctor.

Dr. Mann said with a sunburn like that, Aaliyah needed to get into a dark room immediately. I was really hoping that we could just leave that smelly office and go back up to the hotel. But, according to the doctor, that wasn't what he had in mind for her to heal.

"Even there, the air is too humid, and it is very hot. Since she has sun poisoning, she should not be exposed to heat like that." A lump the size of a soccer ball formed in my throat. I almost jumped out of my skin when my phone began ringing. I stepped outside to talk to Delaney. I was so done with everything. Sitting in this ninety-degree doctor's office that smelled like fish, watching my blood-red sister be examined by Dr. Mann, who talked loud enough to make a person go deaf.

"WHAT do you need, Delaney?!" I hissed through the phone. Then I realized how harsh I was being. "Sorry Del, there's some really bad news going on here."

"Oh, I'm just checking in. Haven't talked to you in a while. What happened?" I told Delaney everything. How Aaliyah went missing, the rock wall, getting stuck in the slide, the punch me sign. Then, Delaney cut me off as I was about to say the worst part of it all.

"When you come home on Friday, I could get your family from the airport," she offered. I inhaled a deep breath and told her about Aaliyah's sun poisoning.

"Well . . ." Delaney just quietly waited. "Due to the extremity of the burn, we need to leave today."

21

Voicemails and Videotapes

Aaliyah

Dr. Mann gave us a note, and we booked a taxi to take us to the airport within the next hour. Before anything, we needed to find Mom. Wherever she ended up going. Dad decided to call to tell her about it, but as I figured, Mom didn't pick up. We heard her voicemail through the little microphones. What I heard was traumatizing.

"Hi, you have reached Tammy Harper, a mommy of a perfect baby named Aaliyah-Bubbiya. Sorry I could not get to the phone on time; she is my top priority. I am most likely bringing my booshy-wooshy to school, her gymnastics class, or a play-date. She sure is a busy little one! Leave a message and I will call you back after putting her to sleep in her pretty princess bed. BYEEEEEE!" Wow. Just wow. I looked up. The expression on Dad's face was priceless. I swear to God . . . if anyone besides us heard that, it is going to be the end of me.

"But what about Matthew and I?" Camille said flatly. Dad stood motionless. I was mortified. A tourist took a picture.

"Here, I'll call her," Matthew said all annoyed. "Honestly Cami, I'm sorta glad Mom didn't mention me in that." Mom picked up when she saw it was him.

"I'm at the spa right now de-stressing. What is it you need, Matthew?" Yikes. When Matthew told her about my sun poisoning, I almost thought the phone's speaker membrane would slip out whole.

"THE BABY!!!!!!!!!!!!!!!! DO NOT WORRY, BABY!!!! I REPEAT, DO **NOT** WORRY!!!!!!!!!!!! I WILL SAVE YOU!!!!!!" Ack, my ear! A crowd of curious tourists formed around us to videotape. My burn was BAD. My skin felt like it had been stung by wasps.

A little kid covered in spit and snot holding a bag of bright red cinnamon Mike & Ike's said to his mom, "Is dat girl da red stuff in my candy?"

Camille

In the airport, Aaliyah was in so much pain she needed to be placed in a wheelchair. Mom was paranoid about "The

Baby." Matthew was saying very sarcastically about how that was the best 18th birthday ever. Dad had on a blank look. The poor guy. I personally couldn't wait to just leave. In a few weeks from now, I go back to school to get my teaching credential.

Our flight, of course, needed to have a delay due to winds over the ocean. Jeez. There was even more commotion when a huge party of people booked our flight back home to Vegas because of an emergency. So people who were already booked, like us, needed to give up their tickets for these people in exchange for $250 and a ticket for the 4:00 flight. I would have taken it just for the money, but Mom protested because she wanted to get "The Baby" home ASAP.

Nobody was giving up their tickets. According to these people, they needed to get to Vegas no later than 9:00 P.M for their dilemma. It was already 2:50, and the flight was almost five hours.

We were able to talk Mom into giving up our tickets. We went to the front desk to turn them in and make the trade.

MATTHEW

I don't know when Mom is going to learn, but she took Dad, Cami, and me and went to trade in their tickets for the money and 4:00 flight. Leaving Aaliyah unattended! The floor was not wheelchair accessible, so it's not like she could come anyway. Why couldn't somebody just stay back with her?

When we got to the top floor, the line was so long it made a loop. Standing all the way at the back, there was no way we'd get to the front of the line in less than an hour. *A whole hour. Aaliyah will be down there by herself for a whole hour without any source of communication.* I knew what to do. I went back down to where she was.

"Aaliyah," I said cautiously.

"That's my name!"

"Don't go anywhere, no matter what you do." I rummaged through my pocket.

"Here, if you need to call Mom or Dad, use this. No games! The password is literally just 000000. Watch. Watch the time. If we still aren't back by 4:00, you need to board that red airplane right there," I pointed out the window to our plane. I gave Aaliyah my cell phone.

"Then, hand the pilot this." I gave Aaliyah her plane ticket and passport, then headed up the stairs to catch up. I had a moment with my sixth sense, though.

Don't leave her. My stomach churned.

I shook it off.

Aaliyah

Um, okay . . . now I am just sitting here all alone, waiting for an hour to pass. At four o'clock, I would board the red plane sitting next to me and give the pilot my ticket. It was just an hour away. I tried to keep the thought in my head. *Just watch it. Watch the time. Don't get distracted.* I was tired from the long adventures and fell asleep. #WorstDecisionEver.

* * *

I was awakened when I felt the pushing of my chair. I opened my eyes and looked up to find some dude pushing me around at the front desk.

"Yes, I saw this little one asleep in a corner by the big window. I don't know how she got there, but that's definitely not normal." I was not sure what I should say, but the manager took me back behind the desk and made an announcement over the loudspeaker. I pretended to still be asleep. My family would surely come and pick me up, right? I took Matthew's phone out from underneath my shirt where I was keeping it and checked the time. Oh no.

MATTHEW

"Wait but I can't get on! I've lost my child! Have you seen her? Did a girl with auburn hair and bangs get on?" Mom screamed at the annoyed flight attendant.

"Yes, your daughter is back there! It is time for takeoff!" I let out a breath I didn't know I was holding. Thank goodness! Aaliyah is on the plane! Maybe she *is* responsible. The plane started to lift up from the ground. Once we were high up in the air, I went to the back of the plane to get Aaliyah. We were sitting in the front.

When I saw that girl, though, I knew it was not Aaliyah. Yes, she had auburn hair and bangs like Aaliyah, but that did not mean it was her. I ran, screaming to Mom and Dad.

"Mom! Dad! Camille! Aaliyah is not on here! That girl is not Aaliyah!" Everyone on the whole plane was now staring. People got out their cell phones and started taking pictures. We all went ballistic. I shuddered. This news meant that Aaliyah was still back there!

Aaliyah

The situation was hopeless. It was 4:30. I looked out of the window for the big red plane. It was gone. I entered the password and tried to call Mom. Only . . . the service was really, really bad. Mom did pick up, but all I heard was static. New try: text messages. I texted Mom, Dad and Cami: Help me, I am still back here! Please help me.

It was having trouble going through. Nooooo!

I felt really worried. I knew Dad would be mad at me. I thought about the past few weeks and everything I'd done. I almost fell from that rock wall, I pretended to get stuck in the slide, I put the *punch me* thing on Matthew, I stayed under that bed and got the police involved, and now this. I didn't watch the time like I should have. Five bad things. Six, if you counted stealing Matthew's phone in the beginning. Six bad things.

I asked the manager for some help. He said he would do what he can. I was taken into a quiet meeting room with nobody in it. I was curious. The manager walked out and I sat there in a wheelchair, my skin burning. Mom is probably having a heart attack. I could just imagine the look on her face. Hey! Hey! Guess who I am!

"NOOOOO!!!!!   THE   BABY!!!!   THAT   IS   MY BAAAAAAABY!!!!!!! GET THE BABYYYY!!!!!" Ahaha.

22

Frustrated Firefighters

Jacen M. Katt, Fire Department Chief

Well, my department just got another call. There is a missing child at the airport. She is said to have ripped denim overalls and a crazy blonde mom. I wonder who it is?

Lord give me strength. I thought those people were leaving! They can't even leave this place without needing to call 911! I won't rest until these wack jobs leave the island, hopefully for good. I do feel bad for the man, Mike, though. He seems to be the only normal one. He reminds me a bit of myself, in fact.

MATTHEW

Things were getting so chaotic. The plane had taken off, and Aaliyah was still back there at the airport. She must be worried. Mom was really losing it.

"I have a baby back there!" she exploded at the flight attendant.

"Okay, ma'am, we are trying all we can to find your baby. Did you leave her in her stroller or something? And how old is she? Toddler years?" the flight attendant asked. He did not seem amused with my crazy mom.

"No, my baby is eight," Mom barked. The attendant's jaw dropped. Every passenger looked mortified with the stupidity. Dad slapped his forehead. Passengers took out their phones and started taking pictures and videos.

"Okay, we will go back to the airport and try to find her." The other passengers were in picture heaven.

Aaliyah

I knew it was time to take action. Since the service was not working, I needed to ask for help. I got out of the wheelchair that I really only asked for because I was too lazy to walk.

"Excuse me, I'm lost. I think my flight took off without me, actually . . ." The guy looked really annoyed.

"Yes, I heard about that. That was quite irresponsible." Then, his speaker started buzzing and a voicemail came on over his walky-talky. A big red plane landed on the crumbly blacktop below a few seconds later.

Camille

We ran out of the plane door, and Mom was totally leading the chain. Oh for crying out loud.

"WHERE IS THE BABY???????" I am ready to punch my mom and Aaliyah in the face. Then, we saw her. There was Aaliyah. She was okay! I think I could call *that* an adventure!

"Oh Aaliyah," I said. Wow.

"That's my name!"

We boarded onto the plane. Aaliyah was placed in a seat and had a pillow to support her head. I could only imagine how many times she's gone to the principal's office.

Aaliyah

I fell asleep again on the plane. I don't know how long I slept for, but like most times I fall asleep, I wake up somewhere else. This time I was in my bed, under the flowy canopy. Matthew was in there, too. He was sitting at my desk playing on his phone. He didn't even realize that I was awake until I raised my voice and asked,

"What are you doing, you creep?"

"You have been asleep for nearly 15 hours now. I was just coming up to see if you were alive because you never sleep this long, but then I got distracted. Posts of us are all over the internet right now. Memes, videos, you name it! Between the slide, the plane, and the fight at the beach, we've gone viral!"

"It's been THAT long?!" He nodded and opened my curtains, letting the darkness escape. It was sunlight that took its place.

23

That's My Name

One week later

* * *

Delaney

Matthew and I met up at his house to say our goodbyes. Starting college is a whole new chapter of our lives! Matthew and his family were out there waiting for us. Aaliyah's skin was peeling like a banana from the sunburn. Her shiny hair was tied into a complicated twist, secured with a flower band. She wore a lacy pink dress. As I saw the car Matthew and I would drive in, away from Vegas, up to college, the one with that enormous but hilarious dent in it, I got a little choked up.

Aaliyah

Today was the day. Matthew was leaving for good. I was going to be an only child. Mindy and I looked at each other. I could tell she was thinking the same thing I was. *Should we? Should we do the same old prank of climbing into the back of the car and going with them to college? Like we did at the dance?*

No. We shouldn't. Our siblings deserve to go on their own. They've earned a life without us now.

About an hour later, it was time to go. Matthew and Delaney got into the car and rolled the windows down.

"Goodbye, Matthew!!!!" Mom said, a little somberly. Now that Matthew was gone, I was going to have to face her unruly ways on my own. Wish me luck. Everybody was sad about leaving. Except me and Mindy, of course! *Welp, you've got yourself an entire decade of no Matthew,* I said to myself. Matthew nodded us goodbye, and Delaney burst into tears. Then, the most repulsive event I have ever witnessed happened.

Matthew kissed Delaney! EWWWWWW!!!!!!!!! Mindy and I lost our marbles.

Matthew closed the window and started the car. We were all waving back at them as the car with the dent in it and so many memories drove down the street. It turned the corner and disappeared with Matthew and Delaney in it.

Mindy

There goes the car. There goes Delaney. Off to start her new life. I then made a promise to myself.

Every time I think of ice cream, I will think of her. Every time I think of dancing at school, I will think of her. Every time I eat anything with butter in it, I will think of that funny prank me and Aaliyah played on her and Matthew. She annoyed me down to the core, but she was cool. I will keep her on my mind, and not forget about all the fun we had in these nine years we've been together. I will call her as much as possible. I opened my eyes. What was left of our family drove home. I was happy I didn't have to deal with her, but I still would be bored alone all day. Nobody to play pranks on. Sibling love really is something else.

That night, sticking to the Delaney Promise, I picked up the phone and waited for her voice.

Delaney

As we drove through the desert making our way to our new university, we told stories. I told him about the ice cream thing. Matthew told me the story about the airport debacle when they came back from Hawaii. Aaliyah is such a pistol. Mindy is, too! But you know what? That's okay!

Tammy Harper

Yes! Of course I am sad that my son just left, but with Matthew gone, I can now have The Baby all to myself! Oh wait . . . I forgot about the husband . . .

Mike Harper

Well, my only ally has just left. God help me.

Camille

Matthew and Aaliyah aren't always my favorite people ever. They can make me mad, and I can make them mad, too. I want them to know, though, that I'd simply have all these fights with them over and over again if it meant I'd still get to experience the fun!

Aaliyah

"Sibling love is the highest form of love there is." It can also be the deepest hate, but love is more powerful, right? Right???

MATTHEW

Everybody has a name. My main one is Matthew. "That's my name!" If you are lucky enough, though, you could have two. I am lucky. Lucky enough to have two. Yep, BB. The BB of my LS.

The End

2

Gangster Grannies

Aaliyah

Things just kept on getting worse since Matthew came home. That night, when my 21-year-old sister Camille was with us, the five of us sat down on the couch. Mom was enthusiastic while informing us the "good" news.

"Kids, we have a special holiday treat for you!" She squealed. Poor Dad. He just sat there with a sour face, waiting to un-pause the TV.

"So, your Grandma Pearl and Grandma Agnes are coming down to join us for the holidays!" We exchanged worrisome looks, waiting for someone to speak. Before you come at me for not being excited about seeing my Grandmas, let me explain.

It all started a few years ago when both our Grandpas passed away, just months apart. Ever since then, Grandma Pearl and Grandma Agnes sort of just... ganged up. They became best friends, and started doing countless embarrassing acts. Every time they are together, something terrible happens. Not once, not twice, but repeatedly until they finally leave. It didn't always used to be like this, though. My Grandmas were rivals. They both disagreed on how Mom should be raising me. This upset Mom, eventually leading to an entire family issue. I do have to say, Mom's parenting sucks, but it's not worth my grandparents and everyone fighting over it. Whenever those two come, we just cannot wait to get them out.

I'm going to have an interesting birthday, and this will sure be a nutty trip!

Little did I know what was coming...

Camille

Alright, let me get this straight. My little sister is about to turn nine, even though she's got the brain of a two-year-old, my mom still doesn't know how to raise a kid after 21 years of experience, and most importantly, Grandma Pearl and Grandma Agnes are coming to celebrate with us?

Right now, I have no other words.

MATTHEW

Us three siblings sat down in my room. We needed some time to discuss the current situation.

"Aaliyah, you are usually a problem, but at least there is only one of you. Now, with the grandmas coming, there will be three!" I say to Aaliyah.

"I promise, I won't be much of a trouble," She replied. "Because trust me, I know what we're about to go through."

About the Author

Elena Southworth was born on July 1, 2007 in California. Yes, you read that right, she's a teenager. When she was 8, her little brother, Mason, started complaining about how he was younger but wished to be older. To make Mason feel better, she started BBLS, (Big Brother Little Sister), a game where they'd switch ages and pretend to be each other. When Elena was ten, she decided to make the adventures they'd go on in the game real and began writing BBLS the book. She's always been creative, artistic, and has a big imagination, so this book was no surprise! Elena loves piano, dance, and her puppy Boe. One day, she would love to go to MIT as an undergrad and then to Harvard to study medicine. However, she will continue writing to keep kids and their families entertained.

Stay tuned for some more BBLS mischief in the next book, The Harper's Holiday Horror!

Contact information:

www.elenasouthworth.com
Instagram: @elenasouthworthofficial
Facebook: Elena Southworth

Made in the USA
Las Vegas, NV
20 November 2020